Finding Percy

Sabrina Jimenez

Published by sabrina jimenez, 2023.

This is a work of fiction. Similarities to real people, places, or events are entirely coincidental.

FINDING PERCY

First edition. November 27, 2023.

Copyright © 2023 Sabrina Jimenez.

ISBN: 979-8223828785

Written by Sabrina Jimenez.

To my Husband and my kids for all their love and support and to my sisters who have stuck by me no matter what. They are not only my biggest supporters. but my biggest fans. This would have never been accomplished without them.

Intro

As I am standing here on the porch of my home, drinking my second cup of coffee of the morning, staring at the beautiful forest in front of me, I am contemplating how far my life has come from seven years ago. I come from a small town of more cows than people and somehow ended up in a more remote state of solitude.

Growing up I had grand dreams of escaping from the small-town life. Travels through Europe, drinking coffee in the local cafes of Paris. Back packing across the Highlands of Scotland. None of that has happened. I ended up in the rolling greens of Washington. Ironically where it all began.

I grew up in the deep south, but I was born here. I always wanted to come back to visit, but I never thought that I would end up living here again. I thought I wanted adventure, excitement, a life surrounded by people and new things. Funny how things turn out so differently than what you thought you wanted.

Instead, I found solitude, and much to my surprise, I love it. For the first time in my life, I feel at peace. Turns out, once I stopped searching for what I thought I wanted, I found what I needed. Thanks Universe. I hear you now. Stop searching and start living, and you find everything you were looking for.

Chapter 1

I came to Washington to go to college. Besides the fact that it was a great school in my field of study, I guess I was running from where I came from. You couldn't get farther from my hometown unless you skipped the country. Did I have a bad childhood? No. Maybe slightly unconventional, but I definitely wouldn't say that it was bad. When you grow up in a small town you either love it or hate it. I think most teenagers dream of running to bigger and better things no matter where you grow up, but when you grow up in a place where everyone knows everyone it makes your life as a teenager all that much harder.

You can't get away with shit. There is always an adult that knows someone in your family that will rat you out faster than you can talk your way out of anything. If you're overly bored and slightly mischievous this is a terrible thing. I was bored, but I will deny, deny, deny that I was ever up to no good. My mother would probably say something totally different, but she's not here, is she? No. So, I guess you will just have to take my word for it!

Anyway, I digress. I came to Washington to go to school. UW has a great Environmental Studies program. I have always been somewhat of a tree hugger, so it was an obvious choice for me. I had grand dreams of being a pioneer in climate change and saving the planet. I wanted to force the world to open their eyes and realize what humans were doing to the planet, and that the destruction they were causing would ultimately be the end! Oh, to be seventeen again.

I took my grand dreams and put them in my back pocket and shipped myself off across the country before I was even legal. My college experience was an eye opening one. When you come from small town USA and end up in Seattle, it's somewhat of a culture shock. I was used to cows and one movie theater in my entire town and went to a city known for its diversity in art, food, and coffee. Which of course turned out to be my heaven because I may have a mild obsession with coffee. It was a lot to take in.

I went from being well known in my community as the Brainiac, albeit somewhat weird, chick to a nobody instantly. I struggled to find myself and to be the best that I could be. Not to sound like an army recruitment commercial or anything. What I found instead, was that I was delusional. The world is never as it seems when you are seventeen.

Now I feel like I should be spinning in circles singing Dancing Queen. You'll get used to my rambling, just do your best to keep up.

Chapter 2

"**P**ERCY!" "Jesus Freaking Christ! How do you use this stupid thing! UGH!"

I walk into my kitchen after hearing my best friend Daphne sounding like she has had a long night.

"Daph, are you fighting with the French Press again?" She glares at me when I start laughing at her.

"Why can't we have a Keurig like a normal person? Coffee should not be this complicated. It's not right. You should be able to mosey on in, blurry eyed, and just press a damn button and TADA! Sweet, glorious nectar of the gods appears!"

She huffs as she's waving a box of coffee in my face.

I laugh harder at her crazy eyes but decide to be a nice best friend and start boiling some water on the stove in a tea pot.

"It's really not that hard Daphne. I've told you a million times. Just add some coffee grounds to the press, boil some water on the stove, when the water is boiling you pour it over the coffee grounds, and then let it percolate for a few minutes and it's done! And you know why I don't have a Keurig."

"I know, I know! Stupid impact on the environment blah, blah, blah. I'm all for saving the trees and all, but it's coming between me and my first love."

"Dick?" I interrupted her tirade laughing.

"No bitch! Well yes, but no. COFFEE. I work too many crazy hours to not be caffeinated. I'd just stop at Starbucks on the way out, but I'm running late."

Daphne isn't around much. She works in PR, so she is a night owl. Constantly off saving some socialite from ruining her reputation by doing or saying something stupid in front of cameras. We are usually two ships passing in the night because we are on opposite schedules. For her to be up this early she must have some crazy big event to plan for.

"Well go finish getting ready or whatever. I'll just put some coffee in a travel mug for you."

Daphne scrambles off towards her room yelling "Thanks Bitch!" as she slams the door behind her.

She was my first roommate in college. She helped the awkward country bumpkin navigate the big city. She took me under her wing instantly and we have been inseparable ever since. She does well for herself in the PR business so she can afford her own place, but she puts up with my crazy green living because she swears, she can't leave me on my own or the world will chew me up and spit me out. She thinks I am naïve. I'm not naïve. I just choose to not let the opinion of others bother me enough to change who I am.

I'm ferreting out a travel mug out of the cabinet when Panda jumps on the counter. Panda is my raccoon. Yes, you read that right, raccoon. I volunteer at the wildlife center part time, and we rescued her out of a trap in the woods a couple years back. I was the one who spent the most time nursing her back to health, so when we tried to release her back into the wild, she kind of stuck with me.

I had gotten into my car that day to go back home and got the scare of my life. When I was looking in the rear-view mirror to back out of my parking space, I saw her head pop up and she stuck her paw in the air like she was waving to me. I screamed so loud the birds in the trees flew off in a rush. Also almost hit said tree, so it might have been the screeching brakes and not my scream that made them fly off. But that is neither here nor there.

Anyway, I spent an hour trying to get her out of my car and back in the woods, but she wasn't having it. The Director decided that she must have imprinted on me and told me to just take her home with me to see if I could coax her back into the woods when she was less riled up. That was two years ago. Now she is a highly domesticated and very spoiled trash panda. And now you know why I call her Panda.

I thought Daphne was going to kill me when I brought her home. She stood on top of the kitchen counter for half an hour yelling at me to get rid of the rabid animal. I tried to explain to her that it was only temporary. That I was going to get her reintroduced into the wild soon and she wouldn't have to deal with her anymore. We see how well that turned out. Daphne still doesn't like the fact that I have a raccoon as a pet, but she tolerates her mostly now. Until Panda leaves scraps of food in her stilettos. Then Daphne's yelling to get rid of her again. I'm pretty sure Panda knows that Daphne doesn't like her, and she fucks with her on purpose.

Chapter 3

After I got Panda settled with snacks, so she won't rummage through my cabinets while I am gone, and Daphne shot out of the house like her butt was on fire, I decide to head to work. We have a massive case we are working on and I need to put as much time I possibly can into researching the history of the area to even have a hope in winning.

Though I mostly like getting my hands dirty with the actual physical conserving of an area, I also majored in Environmental Law to help with the legal sides of things too. I don't like actually being in court, but I use my expertise to consult on the legal side of our cases. I figured if I was going to fight to save our planet I might as well be equipped to do it from all sides, instead of handing the reigns to someone else when it gets hard. I know, I know that sounds awfully self-righteous, but it's mostly selfish. I just hate to lose.

As I pull into the parking lot of Green Activists, the name is also ironic considering most of us that work here are fresh out of college, I see people running around in a tizzy. I see Carl, my boss, talking to some scary looking dudes that most definitely do not look like they are the type to worry about recycling and I am even more confused.

Though this company houses some of the areas most up and coming pioneers in the Environmental community, things around here really aren't all that exciting. To me, it looks like the kind of place that you would expect a bunch of peace-loving Hippies to work at. The color pallet is very soothing with earth tones everywhere you look, very inviting plush bean bag chairs in the waiting area, soothing music in the background, and incense floating in the air. I'm not complaining mind you, it's one of the reasons why I love coming to work every day, but it makes the appearance of a couple Viking looking dudes standing in Carl's office stick out like a sore thumb. We will just overlook the fact that this IS a place that is filled with peace loving Hippies, and I happen to be one of them.

Any who, I pass Katie S., her full name is Katie Scarlett O'Hara Parks, her parents were clearly obsessed with Gone with the Wind. I mean I am down to fan girl anytime, but giving your kid four names to accommodate an obsession with a fictional character is a bit much if you ask me. She's ringing her hands and clearly looking supremely uncomfortable.

"What's going on Kate?" I stop to ask Kate to see if she has any idea about what is going on before I jump head on into the chaotic scene that is currently playing out in front of me.

She nervously looks at me. "I don't know Percy. Carl got a call early this morning that made him start pacing his office and then all the sudden these big scary guys showed up. And then Carl yelled at me to hold all his calls. Yelled at me! Carl NEVER raises his voice. Much less at me! He knows I can't take it!" She starts biting her nails.

"Ok. Calm down Kate. I am sure it's nothing to worry about. Let me go talk to Carl and find out what's going on."

I give her hand a reassuring pat and make my way towards Carl's office. Hoping poor Kate doesn't have a heart attack before I can figure things out and diffuse the situation. This is not how I wanted to start my day. This place is my safe space, and right now it is not feeling very safe. Someone better have a very good explanation on why my peace is being disrupted!

Walking through the normally tranquil office there is an air of trepidation. Like no one knows exactly what's going on but they all know it's not good. We don't get a whole lot of giant tatted up dudes who come into our office very often. Just by looking at them you can tell they have a military vibe going on. I am definitely curious. Why would the military have any business being in our office? As far as I know, we don't handle anything that is of national importance. Obviously, if you take the current state of our planet. Most people don't give a shit about anything that has to do with the environment.

Carl sees me through his office windows walking through the office. I drop my bag off at my desk as he opens his door and yells "Dr. Percy! In my office, now!"

By the way did I mention I finished school with a PhD? So yeah, I'm Dr. Percy. Super weird I know. It still wigs me out sometimes when I hear someone address me as Dr. anything. But it still makes me puff up my chest in pride. I worked hard to finish my doctorate as quickly as possible. Doubling up on classes and going to school through the summer. I managed to finish my doctorate in just a little over the amount of time that most people finish a Master's. Yeah, I am a nerd, but I wasn't playing around. I had goals and I wanted to reach them. Anyway, back to Carl.

I walk through his office doors, "Jeez Carl. You need to chill. You're going to give everyone in the office an ulcer. They're not used to this tension. Especially Kate, you need to apologize to her for yelling at her by the way. She's totally freaking out. What on earth is going on?"

I ask him as I turn to survey the guests in his office. Holy Moly these dudes are huge. Like I look like a child standing next to them. I mean I'm pretty short in general, but these guys must be over 6 feet tall. I'd bet at least 6'3 or more. And they are all definitely tatted up. One in particular has long hair in a bun and complete sleeves of tattoos. He looks definitely dangerous with a scowl on his face, and he's the biggest one in the room. He doesn't look happy to be here at all. The guy standing next to him is just a little shorter, with a smirk on his face. They look very similar in the face so I would put money on the fact they are brothers. His hair is buzzed military short and has a twinkle in his eye. He's definitely a bit mischievous. Equally scary, but that twinkle puts me a little more at ease. The last dude most definitely was military. His hair is also buzzed short and his posture is ramrod straight. Feet, shoulder width apart and hands clasped behind his back. He was also wearing a disapproving scowl on his face. Like he's surveyed everyone in the room, and we are all found wanting. He's the poster child for a "The Military Wants You!" Ad.

I stood up just a little straighter and turned back to Carl. "Soooo, what's going on? Who are they?" Throwing my thumb over my shoulder in their general direction.

The guy standing ramrod straight takes a step towards me and holds out his hand to shake mine.

"Good morning, Dr. Percy. My name is Lindsey. I am the head of Olympus Security. Please take a seat."

He motions to the chair next to me. I can't help but snicker. Olympus Security, how fitting. He cocks an eyebrow at my snicker.

I cover my mouth, "Sorry! I'm not laughing at you. The name of your security company. Olympus. It's just ironic. My name is Persephone."

Other buzz cut dude snickers too. It makes me like him just that much more. Lindsey cuts him a look and he shuts up quickly and clears his throat. "So, it seems." Lindsey turns back to me. "This is part of my team." He motions to buzz cut, "This here is Paxton and the other is Jaxson." I glance over at the big dude, and he gives me a minute head nod. I lift my hand in a small wave.

Looking back and forth between Lindsey and Carl I ask, "Olympus Security? So, what is a security team doing in our office? We're Environmentalists. Not dangerous work. You guys looking to conserve some land for a new office or something?" I ask that part in a very confusing question. It's the only reason I could think of why they would be here.

Lindsey nods his head in Carl's direction when he looks at him questioningly. "Well, you know the big case you have been working on. The Watterson case?"

I nod in return. "Yeah, I'm fighting hard to save 500 acres. Beautiful piece of land. Some unknown third party hired an attorney to fight me for ownership. I am researching the history of the area to find out how old it is to see if I can go the historical conservation route, but what does that have to do with anything?"

"Good. Good. Well, we may have found out who the third party is..." he trails off.

Lindsey steps back up towards me and leans against the desk. "Does the name Giuseppe Russo sound familiar to you?" I shake my head,

"No, not at all. Should it?"

I hear the guy he called Paxton face palm himself behind me. "Do you even watch the news?" He gets a glare from Lindsey again. I'm seeing a trend.

"No, I do not watch the news. I don't even own a TV." I shrug at the look of disbelief on Paxton's face.

Before he can make another ass comment Lindsey interrupts. "That's ok. What Paxton was so ineloquently trying to get across is Mark Fulkom has been prevalent in the news lately for his suspected activity with the mob. He's a ruthless killer who allegedly (he actually uses air quotations) is the right-hand man of the boss of the Seattle crime syndicate. He's never actually been implicated for any of the murders, probably because he has other people do his dirty work for him, but there's enough information out there about his general whereabouts that they know he is associated with them. They just never have enough evidence to prove it." He pauses a moment.

"Ooooook. I feel like this is supposed to mean something to me. What does this Mark person have anything to do with this office? Why would the Mob have anything to do with anything? Again, we are all peace-loving environmentalists. Most people here are vegans for Christ's sake because they can't even stomach the thought of harming animals. I highly doubt anyone here would be associated with the Mob."

Lindsey clears his throat. Like he is about to drop a heavy truth bomb. Oh no, this is not a good sign. If this scary military dude is nervous to tell me something this is going to be bad.

"Well, it has come to Carl's attention, YOU may."

After about 30 seconds of hesitation, I jumped out of my chair screeching. "What?!? What the hell are you talking about? I sure as shit don't have anything to do with the freaking Mob! I can't even watch horror movies because they scare the shit out of me! I sure as hell am not out there popping a cap in people's asses or however the hell people say it these days! Until now, I didn't know the Mob was a real thing!" I immediately begin to spiral.

I may start to hyperventilate a little. Before I even have time to get another tangent out, Paxton smacks me across the face. "What the fuck is wrong with you!" I yelled stunned. I have never been bitch slapped by a complete stranger before. The big guy Jackson immediately grabs him and shoves him not so gently to the back of the room. All but growling,

"What the Fuck Pax?"

I think I am a little more stunned by the fact that Jaxson finally spoke, and that the deep tenor of his voice made my lady bits stand to attention then the actual slap to the face. Whoa. Who is this dude, and why the hell am I reacting that way to him because he is definitely scary? Not someone that I plan on getting anywhere close to my lady bits. He looks like he eats kittens for breakfast. Jaxson is still shoving Paxton back against the far wall by a massive hand to the chest while I'm contemplating my weird reaction.

"What the fuck is wrong with you. You don't lay your hands on a helpless woman."

He's in Paxton's face and a vein may be popping out of his forehead.

Paxton puts his hands up in the air, "Hey, hey, hey chill out bro. She was going into shock. I was just helping her out. I wasn't trying to hurt her. It worked, didn't it? Look, she's calm now." He points in my direction.

I glare at the both of them. Before Lindsey can even reprimand them like I am sure he's going to by the deep intake of breath I hear, I speak up. "First of all, I am not a helpless woman. Just because I am a tree hugging hippie does not mean that I am unable to defend myself. I was a single woman living in a big city when I first got here. I learned really quick not to be a defenseless woman. I have been taking Krav Maga since my first year of college. That was seven years ago. Second of all, any sane person would be in shock to be accused of having any kind of association with the mob. Again, I must reiterate that I am a tree hugging hippie. I can assure you that I do not know the first thing about the damn Mob. Other than what I have seen in movies like The Godfather and trust me that was enough." I am actually wagging a finger in their direction like an 80 year old grandma nagging hooligans in the street.

Paxton looks sincerely chastised, Jaxson just stares at me unblinkingly, and Lindsey tries to cover up a laugh unsuccessfully with a cough. Lindsey motions me back into the chair.

"Dr. Percy,"

I interrupt, "Percy. Just call me Percy."

He nods again, "Percy then. We are not accusing you of working with the Mob. We suspect that Giuseppe Russo is the third party who is fighting you for that plot of land. Mark Fulkham works for him." I dropped heavily into the chair.

I am starting to get my head on straight and realizing what he is trying to tell me. "Oh shit. What you are beating around the bush to tell me is that I have pissed off the Mob. I have pissed off the mother fucking Mob."

I drop my head onto Carl's desk, hard. He comes over to pat me very uncomfortably on the back as I mumble to myself. I have had some crazy situations in my life, but this is rapidly turning into by far the craziest.

"You know I have been known to get on some people's nerves with my natural tendency to ramble, and me killing the curve in class with my awesome grades, but this is a whole new low for me. Who would have thought I would push buttons hard enough to hit the damn Mob? Oooonly me. Only could I be a freaking Environmentalist, the farthest thing from a badass mobster, and still manage to somehow piss off Vito Corleone." Vito was the head of the Sicilian Mob in The Godfather in case you missed that reference.

I take a deep breath. "Ok, so I am trying to win a case against a known associate of the Mob. Which totally does not make me want to back down by the way. As scary as that is, it is my job to do what I can to conserve what land there is left, and plan to keep doing just that. It still doesn't explain why you guys are here. What does it have to do with you?" By this point in time Carl has sat back down behind his desk and is just observing the insanity that is playing out in his office.

"I called them." Carl succinctly states.

"Ok, why? Why do you think this Mark guy is the third party fighting against me?" I give him a blank look hoping he will get to the point. He opens his desk drawer, pulls out a piece of paper, and slides it over to me.

"Persephone Walters, we know who you are. Give up the Watterson case or we will find you. It won't end up well for you."

is chicken scratched across this piece of paper with some weird symbol at the bottom. It kind of looked like a hand throwing a peace sign.

"This note was stuck to the front door. With a knife." Carl tells me. "I recognized the symbol, but I couldn't remember where. I obviously was a little taken aback by the threat, but it wasn't until I started doing research on that symbol that I really got worried. It popped up in numerous places. All the news sites. That's when I remembered where I saw it. That symbol has been carved into every victim that was suspected of being a Mob hit. They were all cases surrounding Mark Fulkham. So, I called around to some of my affluent friends and they passed me the contact information for Olympus Security. I asked them to come in and assess the situation."

I turned to look at Lindsey. "Ok. So, you have assessed the situation I am assuming. What's the verdict?"

"Well, since you are refusing to drop the case, Carl will be hiring us to be your personal security until the case is finished and you either lose, or I am reasonably assured that you aren't going to be murdered in your sleep. We need to find out if this note really is from one of Mark's flunkies or if this is just some jack ass trying to screw around with you."

I blink slowly. "Reasonably assured. Cute. I feel safe already. Thank you for your concern, but no. I highly doubt all this is necessary. I mean come on, why in the world would I be offed for a stupid piece of land? As far as I know, there isn't even anything on it."

"That's what we plan to find out. It's quite obvious if they are coming to threats already then, they are worried about losing this piece of land. It must be important to them for some reason, and we need to figure out why that is."

"So, you are telling me, for the unforeseeable future, I am going to have one of you guys following me around everywhere I go?"

Lindsey points at Paxton and Jaxson, "Mostly one of these two. I have to run the operation, and though you are our main priority right now, you are not the only case we have. So, while we are finishing up the other cases to be able to focus on you, either Pax or Jax will be with you the majority of the time."

Paxton grins at me and waves, Jaxson just stands there stoically like this is the last thing on Earth he wants to be dealing with right now. I let my head drop back to the desk.

Chapter 4

I try again. "Do you really think this is necessary?" Carl heaves an exasperated sigh.

"Look Percy. I'd rather be safe than sorry. You are a rising star in the Environmental field. You are only 24 and already have a PhD. On top of that, you have only been with us for a year and in that time, we haven't lost a single case. Whether or not this is a serious threat, I'd feel much better if you were protected just until we figure out what's really going on."

I lift my head up at that. "Jeez Carl. Be still my heart. And here I thought you liked me for me."

"I do care for you Percy. That's why I am trying to look out for you, but I haven't gotten this far in life and not learned to protect my assets." He stands up and is walking towards the door like this discussion is over.

Lindsey looks at me as I stand up to leave too and figure out what the hell I am going to do about this mess and directs me towards Paxton.

"Pax will be with you today. Just go about your day as usual and pretend he's not there."

"Oh, like this behemoth of a man will easily be overlooked," I mumble to myself and walk out of the office.

Behemoth he mouths at Jaxson as he follows me out of the office with a beaming smile on his face. Jaxson smacks him on the back of the head on his way out and tells him.

"Just do your job and keep to yourself. No horsing around. And under no circumstances, I mean NONE, do you put your hands on her again!" Paxton shoots him a mock salute.

I go over to my desk and start pulling all the files out I have of the Watterson case. I walk over to the communal table in the middle of the office and start piling them up so I can try to organize them and maybe start finding some answers as to what makes this piece of land so special. I'm still working on this case and plan to win, so I still need to continue my research and find a way to do that. On top of trying to uncover some nefarious deeds being hidden by the mob. I shake my head to myself with that thought.

Paxton is looking over my shoulder and watching me lay the files out.

"What is all this?" he asks.

"These are all the files I have with information in them pertaining to the Watterson case."

He perks up at that. "After you are done doing whatever you are doing, I should probably get a copy of these over to Eddy to see what he can figure out."

"Who's Eddy?"

"He's our resident boy genius. Our tech guy. He can do anything and everything when it comes to computers and ferreting out hidden information." He puffs his chest up a little with that, like it's his own personal accomplishment that he is even associated with some boy genius.

I nod my head like that makes sense. I don't know much about private security, but I've watched some movies. There's always a tech guy. It makes sense Olympus Security would have one too. I still don't know anything about what these guys actually do, but I bet if anyone is going to give me any information at all, it will be Paxton. He seems like a talker.

"So how long have you been a part of Olympus?" I try to sound like it's just an offhanded question and I'm not trying to pry, so I keep rifling through my files.

"About four years. Jaxson and I had a hard time finding a job that we could do after getting out of the military. It's kinda hard to adjust after that kind of life for so long you know. Being a civilian again is weird. We were lucky to meet up with Lindsey through a mutual friend who gave us the job at Olympus. It was a perfect fit. We are able use all the assets we learned in the military and work 'em into our home life."

I was a little surprised Paxton was being so open with me, but I guess I did realize he is the more approachable brother. He's just propped up against a filing cabinet like this is just "another day at the office" for him. Then again, it probably is.

"You do a lot of bodyguard work?" I stopped suddenly. It just hit me. I have a fucking bodyguard. I have a bodyguard because I NEED a bodyguard. Oh.my God. Someone may be trying to hurt me. Like for real hurt me. Why is this just now occurring to me? In all the craziness of this situation, it didn't seem real until just this moment that I am in some kind of trouble. Paxton must have noticed my body language because he straightens up and puts his hand on my shoulder.

"I was wondering when it was going to finally register with you. You have been entirely way too calm to be in your situation."

He gently pushes me back down into my chair and hands me a bottle of water out of a nearby communal fridge. It has a sign on the front that says, "Sharing is Caring". I mentally roll my eyes at that. Bullshit. If sharing was caring someone else in this office can take some of the heat off me and join in the whole trying not to get offed by the mob thing. Seriously though, why am I the only one being targeted. It's not like I am the only person who has ever worked on this case. Lots of people help with the research and shit with cases like these. It's just way too big to handle for one person. That's why we have a" team". As a matter of fact, that's a damn good question.

So, I bring that up to Mister professional over here. "Why am I the only one being targeted? Why do I have a target on my back and not anyone else on the team? Why not the lawyer who is going to be presenting the case in court? I'm just the consultant on the case."

Paxton had a half smirk on his face like he was proud I worked that out on my own. "I don't know darling. That's a good question and one that we plan on finding out."

I lift my eyebrow at the darling comment but otherwise let it go. He seems like he's just a naturally flirtatious kind of dude.

"How does this process normally work?" he asks.

"What do you mean?" My mind is running a mile a minute trying to figure out how the hell I got in this situation.

Whatever this situation really is. I still don't really have any idea what's going on. Besides the fact that apparently my life has been threatened and now I have a babysitter for the unforeseeable future, so I'm kind of distracted.

"Tell me how you work through a case. How does it start, how are you chosen to work on it, lead it or whatever, the whole process?" I push out a hard sigh.

"Well, that's kind of hard to say. Every case is different, so the process is not the same. It depends on the circumstances, the intent, and the desired outcome." He gives me a blank stare.

"Look, I imagine it's very similar to how you guys set up one of your cases. Not that I know much about private security, so I am making a lot of assumptions. You guys work as a team. So, there are people on your team that have specific talents. I assume, who takes what case depends on the need of the case and their specific talents right?"

He nods. "Ok, so it's similar here. You are defending people. We are defending the planet. To us, it is a living and breathing thing. Sometimes we are called in by people who have a private plot and want it restored and conserved. Sometimes we are called in to assist State parks. Simply restoration and conservation. Other times, like this case, we are called in to actively fight for the right to keep a plot of land pure or to keep it in the hands of indigenous people. For historical reasons or simply just because people are needlessly killing the planet for more parking lots than is necessary."

I'm not good with sitting still, so I stand back up to pace while I am trying to get my point across so he can get a clear picture of what we do here. I am assuming it's pertinent to my case. I am doing an awful lot of assuming right now. I hope I start getting some actual answers soon.

"Are you following me so far?" He nods again. I guess he's staying quiet to let me get my thoughts straight. Smart man. I'm easily distracted. I have a habit of going off on tangents.

"I personally like doing dirty work myself. I like to be hands on doing the physical side of conservation. I love the way the soil feels between my fingers. And how it smells when it's freshly turned over. Seeing the transformation on what looks like dead Earth to new growth. It's very satisfying to me. But I don't have a PhD and degree in Environmental Law for nothing either. Usually, everyone here has a specific role to play. Depending on their degree, or passion, they usually have one job. I am a bit more unique because I do both. I can work on either kind of case. But like I said I don't ever appear in court. I just have a unique talent in finding a different way of spinning things to generally win. So, I did the research and give the information to the lawyer to present it court. My face is never out there. That's why I don't understand how I am specifically targeted. I mean I am known in the Environmental community from some scientific papers of mine that have been published. But I highly doubt mobsters are sitting down reading academic articles over a cup of tea."

He chuckles at that. "No, you're probably right. But your name has gotten out there somehow. So, we just must keep going through piece by piece to see where we can find the connection. We will no more when we learn more about this Fulkham guy. To see where that connection is. But that's for us to worry about. So don't stress yourself out over it."

"Don't stress myself out over it? I am having virtual strangers following my every move. Piecing apart my life. I'm going to be constantly looking over my shoulder from now until God knows when because some vague ass threat was stabbed into the door of my workplace by some freaking psycho! You may be used to this high stressed environment, but I am not. I make a point to actively find peace in my daily life. To avoid stress. This is not avoiding stress. This is being dropped ass first into big stress. Constant stress. Don't tell me not to stress. This is crazy!"

I may be slightly hyperventilating again. His eyes have gotten big. I guess he's not used to unstable, irrational women. He must work with all dudes, and not be in a serious relationship. All men in long term relationships know not to tell a woman not to be crazy because it just makes them crazier.

"Ok. Ok." He's holding his hands up and approaching me like he's approaching a skittish horse.

"I may have phrased that wrong. You are right. No one expects you not to be upset by this situation. All I was trying to say is that we got you. I work with a good team of guys who have dedicated their lives to keeping other people alive. We protect people, and we are good at what we do. I am just asking you to trust in us that we know what we are doing, and we will handle it."

He has grabbed me by my shoulders and has bent down a little bit to look me straight in the eyes, so I know that he believes what he says. It is somewhat reassuring. "You haven't eaten anything all day. Why don't we take a break and get some lunch?"

I didn't think that I would be hungry when I am as freaked out as I am right now, but on cue my stomach growls. Like the mere suggestions of food have made it perk up and make its presence known. I take a deep breath. I am giving my daily yoga breathing techniques some serious practice today.

"Alright, that sounds good. Let me get my purse."

Chapter 5

We headed down the street to my local coffee shop that is also a little deli. It's called The Toasted Almond. Super cute name, right? It is probably the place that I spend the most time in this city. Aside from my obsession with coffee, it's just convenient considering how close it is to work. It usually has a steady stream of locals that have figured out the delicious pieces of heaven that come out of this place, but it's never so crammed that I can't get a quick lunch if I am on a time crunch.

It's super weird having Paxton follow behind me, constantly scanning absolutely everything his eyes can touch as we walk. It puts me on edge and makes me super paranoid. I start getting jumpy at every unexpected noise like someone is going to jump out and try to nab me. His hand keeps twitching like he's going to reach out and grab me like someone is coming.

"Can you please stop doing that!" I huff exasperated at Paxton. He glances over at me.

"Doing what?" He goes back to scanning the area.

"You keep twitching like you are going to reach out and grab me any second. It's making me super jumpy!"

He gives me that stupid little half smirk he keeps giving that makes me feel irrational. "Sorry Darlin' It's just my reflexes. I'm with you for protection. Not out for a leisurely stroll. You can bet your tight little ass that if anything even remotely looks like a threat, I am going to be grabbing you and throwing you behind me faster than a jack rabbit stealing a carrot."

I give him a strange look. "That's an odd metaphor to use." He gives me a nonchalant shrug.

"Work's, don't it?"

"How come you have a way of speaking that sounds like you are from Texas or something, but Jaxson doesn't?"

He laughs at that. "We grew up in Texas. Jaxson just doesn't talk enough for it to be noticeable. He's more of a cave man grunt kind of guy."

Well can't argue there. Jaxson didn't say much in the time that he was with us in the meeting. I did hear him growl a couple times though. Kind of scary, but oddly sexy at the same time. Man, that dude is scary, but he is like a fantasy come to life. Chiseled jaw, massive build, long hair, short, trimmed beard, piercing blue eyes, and tatted up. He reminds me of a Viking with his massive size and deep scowl. He looks straight through you when deems you worthy of his attention. Mmmm. He's more than likely going to have a premier spot in my fantasies. Probably shouldn't tell his brother that though. May be a little awkward. He gives me that smirk again though like he knows where my mind as gone. He makes me want to growl at him from time to time too. Just not in the sexy way. Out of pure frustration. I have just met the dude, but he's made me roll my eyes so many times already I am surprised they have not fallen out of my head yet.

"Have something you want to tell me Darlin'?" See there I go again. Eyes rolling.

"Like what?" He opens the door for me as we make it to The Toasted Almond.

"You got a thing for my brother?" I huff a laugh.

"Please! I barely know the guy. Even less than I know you, and that's not a lot in itself, and what I do know you have told me. In the time that I have been around him he said maybe five words, and none of them were directed towards me at all. Kind of hard to be into someone who hasn't even spoken to you."

"Oh, come on. There are a lot of things you can like about someone right when you meet them. First impressions and all that."

"First impressions? My first impression of Jaxson is that he is one big scary dude." Super-hot scary dude I mutter to myself. Paxton is laughing out loud at me as we make it up to the counter to order our food.

I'm staring blankly at Paxton as he plows through about three different orders of food wondering how the hell a guy this skinny can pound down this much food. I bet he still has washboard abs under that shirt too. He lifts an eyebrow at me.

"What?"

"Don't talk with your mouth full. It makes me want to murder you. I was just trying to figure out how the hell you keep those washboard abs I'm sure you have while eating this much food. I'm not just vegetarian for the animals. My ass gains five pounds if I even look at a piece of cake."

He was smirking at the abs comment but groaned when I said I was vegetarian.

"Please do not tell me you are one of those crazy ass PETA chicks?!?"

It's my turn to laugh at him. "No, I am not a meat eater hater. It really just started off as a healthy thing for me. I have always had a hard time managing my weight. If you're going to be following me around all the time, you'll see. I must work out a minimum of four days a week to not blow back up like a balloon."

I think his eyebrow is going to crawl of his face if he keeps raising it at me. I may start to get offended if he doesn't chill out with the brow. He huffs another laugh at me as his eyes wander down my body.

"Darlin' I highly doubt anything about you is balloon-like."

"Yeah, you say that now. I have lost a lot of weight over the last couple years. I didn't look like this when I started college. I was overweight my whole life, and when I got to college I had enough with my insecurities, so I decided to do something about it. It's been a long road, but it's become a lifestyle for me now, so I have been able to maintain it. It doesn't hurt that with my first big paycheck I took my first vacation since I started my degree and got my extra skin removed. I don't want to throw all that money down the drain by getting fat again."

Through my little tirade he has stopped eating and is staring at me silently. "What?" I ask with my cheeks feeling like they are on fire from embarrassment. I didn't mean to let all that out. Guys that look like him probably do not want to hear stories about former fat chicks. I'm sure it's a major turn off. Not that I am trying to be a turn on to him. I am not interested in Paxton like that. I have a feeling like he is going to be more like a big brother to me than anything else. He shrugs nonchalantly.

"Nothing to be embarrassed about Darlin'. I have major respect for you that you made such a drastic life change and were able to stick with it. I don't look down on anyone for being overweight. Sure, I'd rather see people healthy, but who am I to judge. My working out religiously was more of a life saving measure than being vain. You can't protect anyone if you are slow."

He gets up to throw away our trash and take my coffee cup to get refilled. I guess he has already picked up on my obsession. He holds the door for me as we are making our way back out onto the street.

"Where to now?" He says to me without even looking at me again. It's still freaky having a conversation with someone who is constantly looking elsewhere.

"Back to finish up some work and then back home, I guess. I don't really do much else than that."

He nods, "good, makes our job a little easier. Speaking of, I hate to be the bearer of bad news, but you won't be able to come back here for a while."

He says it offhandedly, but I stop mid step to turn and look at him.

"Excuse me." I must have given him a dark look because he puts his hands up in a placating manner.

"Hey now. Calm down."

"Oh ho ho. Negative ghost rider. You better be coming up with a damn good reason for taking my absolute favorite place from me."

He puts his hand on my lower back to get me to start walking again.

"That's just it Darlin', anybody who knows anything about you knows how often you come to this place. It makes your movements too easy to track. That's the last thing that we want right now. We don't want to disrupt too much of your life, but don't want to give the bad guys an easy target either."

I sigh heavily, because as much as that sucks it makes sense. I don't like how all the sudden I must worry about crazy shit like being able to be tracked. I feel like I have fallen into a Jason Bourne movie all of the sudden. It still makes no sense to me. How did a normal day get so far off track? I really feel way out of my element, and I don't like it at all.

Chapter 6

I'm packing up all my stuff to leave work finally. It's been a really awkward day. I could tell everyone in the office has been talking about me by the silence that follows the whispers when I walk by people talking. Carl had passed by my workspace about one hundred times today shooting anxious looks at me, like I was going to disappear any second. I wonder if he knows how disconcerting that is. How am I supposed to get any decent work done with all the crazy tension? It didn't help that Paxton was bored out of his mind, so he was leaning back in a chair, with his feet on the table, bouncing an Earth shaped stress ball off the wall and driving me batty. I hope every day in the foreseeable future is not going to be like this. It's going to make me dread going to work and that's the last thing that I want. I love my job. Stupid fucking mobsters and their greediness.

I'm walking towards the door when Paxton jumps up and starts following me. "Are you finally done?" he asks a little too excited about that.

"Yes, I am done. I am going home now."

He puts a hand on my shoulder to stop me. "Ok. Go time. Listen, I am going to be following you home. Let me stay behind you at all times. Do not make any stops. Go straight home. Take a different route than you normally take."

I throw my head back and look up at the sky taking a deep breath. It has been only one day, and I am already over this shit. Paxton is not terrible company mind you, but this cloak and dagger shit is not my thing.

Paxton seems to be a great judge of character, or I am just really predictable, because he stops me again before I can open my mouth.

"Please Percy. Just do this for me. There is a method to our madness, and you can never be too careful. I know all this is really frustrating for you and I am sorry for that. I know you were just doing your job and got caught up in some crazy bullshit. Please do not make our job any harder than it must be. There are currently way too many unknowns to take anything lightly."

I know he's serious because he used my name, for once, and I softened a little at his pleading look. "Ok. I hear you. Straight home, no deviations, different route, got it. I'm not trying to be difficult; I know you are just trying to do your job too."

I go to open the door to my FJ Cruiser and get on my way. Well, on our way, I guess. He stops me from closing the door and leans down to look me straight in the eyes before I can put my sunglasses on.

"You are not just a job to me darlin'. I know we have just met, but I really like you and I don't want to see you get hurt." That took me off guard and I didn't even know what to say to that, so I just nodded. He lets me close the door and jogs to his vehicle. It's a black inconspicuous SUV of course.

I sigh and feel my shoulders relax as I step into my home. Paxton is close on my heels again observing everything.

"Well, this just made things interesting."

I look back as I walk into my kitchen to make yet another cup of coffee. "What do you mean?"

"Your house is beautiful, but not very defensible. We need to up our security game. You basically don't have a security system and you are very isolated, surrounded by open land and then woods. Lots and lots of woods. Too many easy places for a person to hide. Why the hell are you all the way out here on your own?"

Chapter 7

Paxton insisted on helping me cook dinner. "You are my bodyguard, not a maid Pax. I got it. Just sit down."

All I can see is half his body sticking out of the fridge, but he didn't say anything so I can only assume he is shaking his head with the slight wiggle of his body. Before I can say anything else, the front door bursts open. Paxton immediately whirls around and has his gun drawn at the intruder. Unfortunately, that "intruder" is my roommate and I just realized that I have not had time to update her on the situation.

Her purse thumps as it hits the ground and she throws her hands in the air and screams, "What the fuck!"

Paxton immediately lowers his gun and puts it back up when I yell, "Paxton! No. It's fine. It's just Daphne, my roommate."

Daphne slowly closes the door and picks up her purse, eyeballing Paxton like he's a threat.

"What the fuck Persephone! Who the hell is this and why did he just draw a gun on me! Since when do you hang out with guys with guns? Miss make love, not war!"

That gets a snicker out of Paxton, even though his back is turned to us and he's finishing dinner. He's trying to give us some semblance of privacy even though he's still in the same room.

"Sorry Daph! It's been a crazy day. A lot has been going on and I have not had time to update you. You're home early. Let me pour you a glass of wine and we will sit down, and I will explain everything."

It took a couple of glasses of wine to get everything out and in the open. Daphne is sitting here staring at me with a stunned look on her face. I have never seen her this quiet before. It's disconcerting. She finally seems to snap out of it.

"Let me get this straight. You. Persephone Walters. Is being threatened by the Mob. The motherfucking Mob? How is this even possible. You are the least aggressive, most kindhearted person I know. This is ridiculous." She turns to look at Paxton. "And you are part of a private security team that is going to be following her around 24/7 until this shit is figured out?" Paxton nods. "Do they all look like you?"

Paxton's brow furrows and he looks at me confused. I just shrug, because I know where this is going, and I am trying to keep a straight face.

"What do you mean?" he asks Daphne.

She slowly looks at him up one side and down the other. "You know. Does your whole team look like you? Are there going to be nothing but big, sexy, pieces of man meat all over my house all the time now? Because a girl needs to be prepared for this. It's not that easy looking like this all the time. It takes work, and I want to make sure that I am fully prepared in the a.m. if you guys are going to be around all the time."

I lost it at the absent blinking look on Paxton's face. He is getting a crash course in my best friend right now and it is highly entertaining. I do not think Pax has ever met someone that was on the same level as him before, not a woman anyway, and he has no idea that she will chew him up and spit him out. I have seen her do it dozens of times.

Daphne is not a bad person, or a skank. She is just on a very aggressive road to finding her one true love. She is not one of those cynical serial daters that has a different man every week because she hates commitment or anything. She very much believes in true love. She has parents that have been married for forty years and are still very much in love, and she wants that. She's doing everything she can to find that, so she kind of goes through men rather quickly. It's a, you don't buy a vehicle before test driving it, kind of situation.

She is absolutely gorgeous though, so none of them complain. Daphne is tall, blonde, with a runway model body. She is always completely made up and dressed to the nines, no matter where we are going. There is a reason why her firm is one of the top P.R firms in the area. She knows what she wants, and she knows how to present herself to get it too.

Paxton finally gets his bearings and looks at me and whispers, "I think I'm in love. I mean, I thought I was going to chase you hardcore, but nope. I just found my soul mate."

It makes me snicker because he has no idea what he's getting into. Maybe Daphne is going to be super useful in this situation after all. She will be able to help distract Paxton and give me a second to breathe without someone up my ass all the time. I haven't even been able to pee in peace today. It's super awkward trying to pee when you know there is a grown ass man leaning against the door probably able to hear everything.

I slip off to take a shower and relax for a minute while they are talking. My paranoia is still getting to me, I creep in slowly to my spacious bathroom to make sure no one is hiding in there. Paxton checked the house before he let me go in, but I still remember his comment about someone being able to hide easily out here. Satisfied that it is indeed empty, I jump into the shower to soak away this insane day.

After I'm done and dressed in some comfy sleep shorts and a warn t-shirt, I go back out to the dining room to see if Pax and Daph are still where I left them. On my way out of my bedroom I hear another male voice that is not Paxton. A voice that makes all my insides shiver in pure lust. What is Jaxson doing here?

"What the fuck are you doing Pax? Where is Persephone?" I guess Paxton had a terrified look on his face because Jaxson continues," Yeah, that's what I fucking thought. You're here to protect her. How are you going to protect her when you are out here fucking around and have no idea where she is?"

That's the most I have ever heard him speak. The only other time was him griping at Paxton too.

"I'm right here, and completely fine. I just went to take a shower. You don't need to rip his head off. He checked the house before he let me come in. No one is here. He does not need to follow me around like a lost puppy when I'm in my own house. So, take it down a notch. Don't murder him just yet."

They both get really quiet and are just staring at me. I look between the both of them and look down at me to make sure that all my bits are covered.

"What? Why are you staring at me like that?"

Paxton stands up and clears his throat while walking over to me. He's a look on his face that makes me take a step back. I ask, "What" again starting to get a little nervous.

Chapter 8

"You have tattoos." Paxton starts circling me.

"Yes. Why? You are acting like that is crazy." I point to both him and Jaxson. "You guys are both covered in tattoos, why are you so surprised that I have them? You aren't those guys that think that women shouldn't have tattoos, are you? Because that's ridiculous. I get that enough from my family. Don't need it from you."

My hands are now on my hips in indignation.

He shakes his head; Jaxson is still just staring at me silently barely blinking. Daphne rolls her eyes and stands up to refill her glass.

"No. It's because it is always very unexpected for people to see the number of tattoos that you have hiding under your hippie façade." She laughs.

"What's that supposed to me?" I turn to look at her.

We've never really talked about my tattoos. They have never seemed to bother her, so I'm surprised this conversation is just now coming up.

When I started "finding myself" in college, I discovered how much I loved tattoos. I have always been a somewhat creative person and I loved that I could express that through artwork on my skin. It was always very cathartic for me. I wasn't the type of girl that cut my hair, or anything like that, after a breakup or big life change. I got tattoos. When I was struggling with not being scared to just be who I am, it always felt good for me to put a piece of that out there for the world to see. It helped with my convictions. So I have quite a few now.

Paxton stopped circling me like a freaking shark but was still staring at me.

"It just doesn't fit. You are so sweet. It just surprised me that's all. How many do you have? It looks like you might have more than I do. Maybe even rivaling Jax over here."

I rolled my eyes at him again. "Girls can have a lot of tattoos too. And what the hell? I must be a bitch to have tattoos. That's a bit sexist don't you think? I don't really know how many I have in total. I haven't counted them. There's more that you can't see though." Before he opens his mouth, I see the gleam in his eye. Apparently, Jaxson does too because he smacks him upside the head again.

"No. I am not going to show them to you either. Those are just for me. Some of them you must see me pretty much completely naked and that is not going to happen!"

He's been staring at my leg piece that covers my thigh and disappears into my shorts. It goes all the way up my hip, but he can't see that. I guess I should have rethought the short shorts. I am just not used to having to worry about what I am wearing at home. It's usually just me and Daphne and she has seen my naked hundreds of times.

"What kind of flowers are those? That piece is badass. You have a damn good artist. How big is it?" Jaxson takes another step closer to him like he's going to pop him again. "Hey! I'm just curious. You know, from one tattoo wearer to another. I don't mean anything by it."

"It's fine. That one is pretty personal, but since I have already told you a little bit about my story it will make sense. Those are lotus flowers. They symbolize rebirth or rising above suffering. It covers my whole outside thigh and winds up to my hip. I get a new flower added onto the vine whenever I start falling back into old habits and want to remind myself who I am again. That has happened a lot."

Wanting to change the subject, and a little unnerved by Jaxson's silence, I turn to him and ask him.

"What are you doing here anyway? I'd ask how you knew where I lived but I guess that would be a stupid question. I thought this was Paxton's time to babysit me. Has something happened?"

He blinks at me a few more times, but gestures for me to sit down. Which shoots my nerves to an all-time high.

"I'm here to relieve Pax. He needs to get back to the compound to be filled in by Lindsey. He needs him to investigate a couple things that are under his expertise. I am taking over for a while. There's nothing for you to worry about. Some things must come to light in the investigation."

He holds up his hand to stop my rapid-fire questions that are wanting to come out. "I assure you there is nothing for you to worry about just yet. We have it all under control and will continue unraveling everything we can. When we know more, we will fill you in."

His voice is gravelly. Like it needs to be warmed up from lack of use. I can hear the very subtle Texas twang under it though. Not as strong as Paxton's, though I am pretty sure he does it on purpose to sound more inviting, but it's just there.

"Look, if something is going on, I want to know. I am not some damsel in distress. I am not going to freak and pass out or some shit, you don't need to handle me with kid gloves. I don't appreciate being kept in the dark when this involves my life."

I guess people don't usually argue with Jax because Paxton whispers "ooooh shit" and makes his way out the door. Daphne also disappears, leaving me and Jaxson alone in the kitchen.

"Why don't you give me tour of the house, and I will tell you what I know."

He takes a couple steps closer to me and I have to look up to look him in the eye now.

"I don't think you are a damsel in distress, and I am not trying to handle you with kid gloves. I just don't want to stress you out unnecessarily when we don't have all the facts yet."

The sincerity in his eyes takes the winds out of my sails a little bit. "Alright, let's see the house."

Chapter 9

I took him to walk the perimeter of the house first so he can get a feel for the location and layout and all that. He was eyeing everything while we were walking just like Paxton does, but he seems a bit more intense about it. I guess because Pax still maintained conversation while he does it. Jaxson is silent mostly, just asking questions here and there.

He is looking up at the roof of the house with his head cocked to the side. "Are those solar panels?"

"Yes. Those were one of the very first additions I made to the house when I first bought it." I was extremely proud of myself for buying my first house, but ecstatic about the fact that I made enough to make it how I wanted and was able to afford solar panels. They are expensive at first, but they save so much energy and money in the long run. I rarely have an electric bill.

Even with the mostly overcast skies Washington sports, we still get enough sun peeking through that it charges my house constantly. I don't use that much electricity in general though.

We walked around back to explore that part of the house and he stopped in his tracks when he saw the crazy contraption back there. Can't blame him though, most people find me extremely weird when they see this part of my lifestyle. Which is why I don't have many guests over. My last ex was the straw that broke the camel's back on that one.

I stood there in silence just waiting for him out while he wandered around my backyard checking everything out. My first impulse is to fill the silence. I get chatty when I'm nervous and tend to ramble, and

Jax definitely makes me nervous, but I have a feeling that it would just irritate him, so I stay quiet.

He finally walks over to my water collection system and is looking very confused. He finally looks over to me and asks, "This looks like some sort of water system, but what do you use it for? I know you have running water in your house because you took a shower."

I can't help but giggle a little. "Of course, I have running water. I am environmentally conscious, but I still like my comforts. This is a collection system that I use to water my plants and wash my clothes.

It collects the rainwater and stores it in those bins so I can use it in my wash bin over there. I point to my old school wash bin.

"You wash your clothes by hand outside?" He gives me an incredulous look.

I look a little sheepish. This always ends up being an awkward conversation. I huffed a little. This is why I don't bring a lot of people over to my house. It makes me look nuts.

"Yes, I wash my clothes by hand, yes I have solar panels, yes I try to grow as much of my own food as possible," I gesture to the back part of my yard that is neatly planted rows of all kinds of different vegetables and herbs. "I am an Environmentalist. Don't you think it would be slightly hypocritical if I didn't?"

He stares at me unblinking but gives me a small curt nod and keeps walking.

He makes his way over to my sanctuary. Most people who have luxurious backyards have t.vs, and lush furniture, or expensive outdoor kitchens and grills. I have my own little fairytale wonderland.

I have several large trees in my backyard. Hangin all through them are twinkly lights. I have tiki torches throughout the area, and a large circular garden chair hanging from the largest tree in the corner. It has large, lush pillows, and it is my absolute favorite place to hang out.

There is a massive amount of fragrant colorful flowers all over. When I sit back here, and I do often, It just makes me feel like if I sit really still and really quietly I would be able to see little fairies flitting from flower to flower. I know it's childish, but it makes me feel calm and peaceful.

Jaxson really doesn't say much as he looks over everything while he is slowly stalking my yard like a predator waiting to jump on anything that makes a sudden movement. But there is no movement. It's calm and quiet and all you can hear are the crickets in the background. I wonder if he is silently judging me, but he makes no sign of what he is thinking.

Gah! This dude is like Fort Knox.

"Alright, I have seen the perimeter, now take me through a thorough tour from the inside. Every room, every closet, every place that someone can hide. I need to know it all." Jaxson barks.

"Well ok then. It's pretty sad when the only time I hear you speak is when you are barking orders. I believe that's the most I have ever heard you speak in general. It's a sexy voice. You should use it more often. I mean not sexy. Sorry, that's awkward. Well, it is sexy, but that's not the point. Ugh, never mind! Just come this way"

I'm pretty sure my face is as red as it feels right now. His lips did curve up a little though. So I think that was a smile. His version of a smile anyway. That's progress. I still keep my head down and walk quickly to my back door. I can see Panda sticking her face in a window in the kitchen trying to be nosy. I glare at her so she will get off the counter. Not that she will listen to me anyway. No one does. I inwardly huff.

"My house is mostly open. There are not a whole lot of nooks and crannies. I like the spacious open vibe. I think it makes it feel less cramped and the energy is better. Pointing to the right. "This is supposed to be the laundry room, but obviously you have seen that I wash my clothes outside, so I just turned this into a mud/storage room."

It's a small room, but I had shelves built in and hooks put up, so it's still organized and easy to clean. When we walk straight ahead, we come into the main part of the house.

"The majority of the house is right here." I point straight ahead. "That's the front door obviously. You have seen the wrap around porch. As you can see everything else is open. The kitchen and living room."

I see his eyes roaming all over the rooms. Realizing what I said is true. I really do have a very open house. It's quiet, and easy to hear Daphne's music in her room. She has a tv in there, but I don't have one in the living room. I don't really watch tv and I made that wall pretty much one giant window so during the day you can open the curtains and have an amazing view of the land and forest.

Earth tones are pretty much how my house is all decked out. Kind of my thing obviously. I have all low lying furniture and some bean bags in there, a bookcase with my books and keepsakes, a couple tables, but not a whole lot. I like the minimalist feel and the cleanliness. It makes me happy.

I can see him staring at the major feature in the room. It's what everyone sees first. The room has all its natural beams, almost like a log cabin feel, but in the corner and over the ceiling is a tree. I had the builders keep some of the natural wood and they carved a tree literally into the side of the inside of my house. It spans from floor to ceiling and halfway along the ceiling. It's a big tree, and my absolute favorite part of the house. I even had them cut a hole towards the bottom and that's where Panda lives.

He looks over and raises an eyebrow at me. "Yes, yes, I have a tree inside my house. I know it's unusual, and most people think it's weird, but I love it, and it's Panda's home." I just kind of trail off and shrug.

He looks at me and I think he was just going to ignore me again, but to my surprise he looks me straight in the eyes and says, "It's beautiful work, and it fits for you. It's original, but not weird. Let's continue."

Well ok then. I showed him the rest of the house. There wasn't much else besides the bedrooms and a couple of bathrooms. When he finishes cataloging every nook and cranny, we make our way back to the kitchen.

Chapter 10

"Paxton made dinner. Are you hungry? I'll have to warm it up, it looked great though. He made curry and lentil stew. I hope you don't mind vegetarian."

"Paxton cooked for you?" he asked incredulously.

"Yeeesss... is that odd?"

Jaxson shrugs. "He usually doesn't cook much. He must really like you. No, I don't mind vegetarian, and yes I could eat."

He goes into the kitchen to grab some bowls and starts ladling up some of the stew. I found it kind of odd that he knew exactly where they were. I must have had that showing on my face, or staring at him oddly because when he looks at me again, he pauses.

"I'm getting to know you. As much as a free spirit you are, you are also logical. Seemed like you would be organized that way too. It made sense."

He shrugs again and motions me back over to the table. I sit down awkwardly. I have gotten used to Paxton, but I am not sure how to act around Jaxson yet. He's so intense and quiet, it makes me squirm. For more than one reason. Now that I am able to look at him more thoroughly without being distracted by my freaking out, he is even sexier than I originally thought.

He has smooth tan skin and is a little bulkier than Paxton. You can see his t-shirt stretch over the bulges of muscle. He has his dirty blonde hair up in a "man bun" and his eyes are a deep blue that look like oceans are swimming in them. He doesn't twitch with my obvious staring, but his eyes sink into a slightly darker shade. OOOh the things I would like to do to this man, and how I'd love to drown in those baby blues.

I stop my staring, dig into the food, and pour myself another glass of wine. I moan a little about how good it is. That makes him twitch a little. Still not sure if it is with interest or annoyance yet though. It's hard to tell with his silence.

Do I keep my mouth shut or do I try to make conversation? I think he may just grunt at me. I decide to hell with it, I'm going to dig a little. I bet he will at least be willing to talk business.

"What was your assessment on the house? You never said what you think."

He takes a minute to get his thoughts together, or at least I hope that's what he is doing, and not outright ignoring me. There is nothing that I hate more than being ignored. Tell me to shut up, tell me to go away, but do not ignore me. It gets me fired up really quick. I quirk my eyebrow at him, waiting to see if he is going to respond. Finally, he sets his water glass down. I offered him some wine, but he wouldn't take it. I forgot I'm at work. He's not here to socialize.

"You have no security. You have a lot of open land, so we would be able to see anyone coming up to the house, but there is a lot of coverage in the trees for them to hide and take time to get in place before we even noticed them. So, it would be very easy to get caught off guard. I will be sending Eddy over, when he gets the chance, to put a security system in place."

I sighed. "Yeah, Paxton pretty much said the same thing. I didn't renovate the house with defense in mind. I never thought in a million years I would be in this position."

He softened a little at that. I probably look a little defeated. Which I guess is appropriate for the situation because I feel defeated. Not enough for me to quit trying to win this case, but enough for me to chug the last of this glass of wine and refill it. I deserve a minute to throw myself a little pity party. It'll be a party of one. Paxton left,

Daphne is doing what she does, and I sure as hell won't get any pity from Jax. There's no one else. Wow, how sad is that. Ugh, wine it is. Wine never leaves me lonely. I snicker to myself at that.

I've had an entire bottle of wine and am swaying to music in my head. Jaxson had gotten out a laptop and had been pounding away at the keys, so I almost forgot he was there. I am startled a little when I look over and he is leaning against the counter watching me. I trip over my own feet and stumble. He catches my elbow before I completely fall over though. That makes me giggle. He raises an eyebrow at my random giggling.

"Bodyguard. Haha. You're my bodyguard but saving me from myself." I giggle again. He takes my now empty glass and sets it on the counter.

"Ok. Kitten. I think it's time for bed."

He starts to maneuver me towards my bedroom. I may or may not sway a little on my feet.

"Kitten? I'm not a damn kitten. I'm a tigress. Rawr!" I'm trying to be sexy and mime scratching in the air, but I'm pretty sure I'm just coming off crazy. He does chuckle at that. I made Jax chuckle! It's a sexy as hell deep rumble too that I felt all the way to my lady bits.

He gets me into the bedroom and starts to take off my shoes, when he unbuttoned my jeans, I jump back and put my hands up. "Woah woah woah there buddy! You have to buy me dinner first! Well, we just had dinner, but that's beside the point! You can't just jump right into taking my clothes off right after we meet no matter how sexy you are." While waving my pointer finger at him in the air it jostled me enough, I started to tip over. "Shit!" He catches me again.

He chuckles again standing me upright. "I'm not trying to do anythin' untoward Kitten. I'm just tryin' to help you get undressed and ready for bed, so you don't kill yourself in the process."

I just blink at him for a second. His accent just came out and he sounded a lot more like Paxton for a second. He's coming back towards me with his hands up just like Paxton did, making me think of a skittish horse. I snort to myself. Horse. Stallion. I bet he's a stallion in the sheets. I almost trip again. Damn it.

He makes his way back over to me slowly and starts sliding my jeans back down so I will stop tripping over them. I start rethinking telling him to back off, because the way he is staring at my thigh piece is super hot.

He runs his finger over one of the lotus flowers and murmurs, "These are beautiful. You have a very talented artist."

I'm distracted by his touch, so I just mumble unintelligibly "Uhhuh, yep." He's touching my calf muscle now. He noticed the mosaic feather I have on my left calf. His scrutiny is making me squirm again.

He finally gets my pants off and drops them into a laundry basket I have in the corner. While his back is turned, I rip my shirt off over my head intending to take my bra off and put it back on, but he's stopped in his tracks, and I can feel him staring. I completely forget that I'm just standing there in my bra and underwear, and I turn around to see what made him stop. I'm sure it'll be really awkward tomorrow when I have to look him in the face sober. I'm not usually this comfortable around anyone half naked. Being overweight the majority of your life does that to you. I guess I can thank that one on the wine.

He takes a slow step towards me. His intense stare makes me take a step back. I feel like I'm standing in front of a predator, and I am the prey.

"What are you doing?" I finally managed to huff out.

"Relax Kitten, I'm not going to touch you. I just want to look at your tattoos. I know Daphne said that you were covered in them, but I thought she was exaggerating."

HE SLOWLY MAKES A CIRCLE walking around me. "Tell me about these. Do they mean something, or did you just pick them out of a catalog?"

"Some have specific meaning. Some are just things I like. I already told you about the lotus flowers. The feather I just like. "The arrow", I point to the inside of my right forearm, "reminds me to keep moving forward and don't worry about my past. The Hamsa hand", I point at the inside of my left forearm," is a sign of protection and wards against evil. The owl", I point to my right shoulder, "is a symbol of wisdom and sometimes of death so that's kind of a play on my name and I just happen to love owls. That", pointing to the heartbeat over my left breast, "was that last echocardiogram of my grandmother's before she died." I lift my left arm, along my ribs is written "To thine own self be true", "this is a promise to myself to not give a shit about what anyone else thinks of me and to just be true to who I am."

I turned around and showed him my back. I have a massive Tree of Life between my shoulder blades. "That should be self-explanatory."

I turned back around to gage his reaction. He seems kind of stunned at first, but then just grabs a shirt off of the chair and puts it over my head, holding me still while I put my arms through the holes. He helps me into the bed and just nods and walks out of my room.

"That man and his Fort Knox attitude is infuriating." I grumble to myself as I'm falling asleep.

Chapter 11

OOOOh God. I grumble as I roll over. I should not have drunk all that wine last night. I smell coffee. Oh, sweet baby Jesus I need some coffee. As I am rolling out of bed and walking to the door it hits me. Coffee. Daphne doesn't know how to make coffee. It must be Jax. Last night. Oh, dear god, last night's memories roll through my head like a rolodex of bad decisions. I groan. Note to self, do not drink around Jaxson. I just make a fool of myself. Though in retrospect it could have been worse. At least I didn't end up completely naked and throwing myself at him.

I turned back around to throw some yoga pants on before I walked into the kitchen. He saw everything last night but better try to keep things less awkward for the both of us.

I sniffed hard as I walked up to the counter. Mmmmm coffee. Before I can even make a move towards the french press, Jax slides a cup to me. I quirk an eyebrow at him.

"Pax may have mentioned your slight obsession." Jax smirks as he watches me all but guzzle the entire cup in 2 seconds flat. I may or may not moan a little. I can't help it. Besides chasing the fog out of my head, it always gives me that little jolt the first thing in the morning that I need to get my day going. I am not really a morning person. Ok, I am not a morning person at all.

Luckily, Jaxson doesn't say anything at all about last night as he turns his back to me and gets back to whatever it is that he is cooking on the stove. Which smells delicious by the way. I didn't notice it at first because I had zeroed in on the coffee. My bad.

"I made you an omelet. I am assuming since you had eggs in the fridge that you are not vegan and that's ok. "Jaxson places a plate down in front of me on the breakfast bar.

"It smells fantastic, thank you. And yes, I am vegetarian, but not strictly vegan. I do eat eggs and cheese and milk. Just not any meat specifically. Again, thank you for your thoughtfulness. Most people are annoyed by my eating habits."

Jaxson just quirks an eyebrow at that. He's standing there looking at me like he wants a response but doesn't say anything. It's slightly annoying. I am not fully awake yet and haven't had my second cup of coffee to try to play the "decipher Jaxson's facial expressions game". So, I give a very mature response. I just quirk my eyebrow back. If he doesn't want to talk, fine. I'm not going to waste energy trying to drag responses out of him.

I gobble up the rest of breakfast, pour myself another cup of coffee, and make my way back towards my bedroom to take a shower and get dressed for the day. I don't have to work so I need to figure out what I am going to do with myself. That is, if they even let me do anything.

Ugh, let me. I am a grown ass adult and being held all but prisoner because some jackass Italian wants to be a dick for no reason. I've gone past being afraid to just being annoyed now. Nothing else has been said, no one has made any moves against me. I feel like everyone's time and resources are just being wasted on me. I really think it was just some lame threat to scare me off, I highly doubt anything is going to come of it.

I am musing to myself as I am turning on the shower and laying clothes out when I hear a throat clear behind me. Which makes me all but jump out of my skin.

"Jesus fucking Christ!" I try not to smack Jaxson when I see that he is fighting a losing battle of trying to keep a smile off his face.

"Sorry." He clears his throat again. "I was just trying to let you know I was here and to try not to scare you. You are very jumpy."

I give him a blank look. "Jumpy? Of course, I am jumpy. Besides the fact that I was just running through everything that has been going on in my head just then, I am also not used to having company. Besides Panda, I am usually alone."

He loses the smile on his face with that comment. I don't know why it seems to bother him so much. It doesn't bother me. I mean, of course there are times every now and then that I get a little lonely because Daphne is gone all the time, but I just do something to keep myself occupied then, and those times are few and far between. I am mostly content with my solitude. I don't have anyone but myself to answer to. With the few exes in my past that were very controlling and didn't like my independence, it's a nice change. Probably also why I am still single. I inwardly shrug to myself. Oh well, I am happier for it.

"I am not going to let anything happen to you. You are safe with me." Jaxson gruffly responds finally.

"I know I am. I'm really not worried about being attacked in my own home. I was just lost in thought and wasn't paying attention to what's going on around me. It's a common habit for me unfortunately. I am always lost in my own head. But I guess that means that you are with me today?"

I am kind of awkwardly standing in my bathroom while the water runs, but since he never really says anything, I don't want to kick him out while he's being chatty. I like the sound of his voice.

"Yes. I am with you today. When you get out of the shower we can go over the schedule for today."

With that, he does an about face and he stalks back out of my room.

WE HAVE GOTTEN A SORT of schedule down. It is a constant revolving door of Paxton and Jaxson (on occasion Lindsey) switching off, taking turns watching me. It feels like it's been forever and nothing new has happened. I am still going about my days as usual so far, with adjustments here and there when Jaxson doesn't like my idea of being out and about too much. Daphne tried to get me to go out with her once and I thought Jax was going to have a coronary. The only time he doesn't complain much is when we go to the gym. I think he likes using that time to blow off steam. Whether it's from the lack of action, or me irritating him, I don't know yet.

I am still going about my normal day as usual, so when I get out of the shower, and I hear multiple male voices in the kitchen I am curious. I get dressed quickly to find out who it is. When I walk into the kitchen it is full of all the impossible males in my life currently and one, I don't know.

Jaxson is leisurely leaning against the kitchen counter not saying anything, ever the observer, Paxton and Lindsey are facing off arguing about God knows what and then there is a good-looking guy I have never seen watching them and occasionally laughing at what's being said.

He's tall and lean, caramel colored skin, short black hair on the sides but it's a little longer on top so it flops into his face when he throws his head back and laughs. He's wearing glasses. He is not as covered in muscle like the other men, more like a swimmer's body. He doesn't carry himself as harshly as the other guys. I would bet this is their tech guy Eddy.

He is the first one to notice my entrance. He looks up and lifts his eyebrows when he sees me.

"Aye Mami! Now all the overtime makes sense!"

Paxton smacks him in the stomach. He makes an umph sound, but instead of castigating him, he throws his head back and laughs. A full body laugh. It makes me smile along with him. This guy is the life of the group. I thought Paxton was the fun loving one, but now I can see that this one lives for the adventure.

Jaxson glares at him, Lindsey has a flat look on his face, and Paxton takes a step in between us and flaps his hand in his direction. "Darlin', this is Eddy, Eddy this is Persephone. Our newest case."

That makes me quirk my eyebrow at him and my stomach falls just a little. I mean, logically I know that I am a job for them, but I thought Paxton and I at least we're kind of friends now. I cleared my throat and took a step towards Eddy to offer him my hand.

"Hi Eddy, I have heard a lot about you. I'm Persephone, but most people call me Percy."

Instead of taking my hand and shaking it, he flips it over and brings it up to his mouth as he bows slightly.

"Ah, Persephone. I have heard, oh so much, about you and it is a pleasure to finally meet you. I very much look forward to working this case and being of service to you anyway that I can."

He winks at me and jumps backwards. He seems to know that he was about to get smacked by Paxton again. He dodges and light footedly hops out of the way and runs out the door laughing. It makes me smile. I don't get to see Paxton grumble much, so it makes my heart a little lighter to see their dynamic.

All the men are staring at the door with their arms crossed like they can mentally smack Eddy upside the head. I clear my throat to get their attention.

"Well, he seems like a character."

Slowly they all turn back to me. Paxton drops his arms and comes to sweep me in a hug and spin me around. "That he is. He doesn't get out of his cave much, so excuse his lack of social graces. He's harmless." I pat his chest as he puts me back on my feet. "It's fine. He doesn't bother me. I like to see that at least someone keeps you on your toes and knows how to keep things light. You guys are too serious sometimes." I turn towards the kitchen and Jaxson must have read my mind, because before I even take two steps, he is handing me a full cup of coffee.

"Thanks. I guess you have easily figured me out. Ply me with coffee and I stay happy as a clam."

One side of his lips quirk just a little and that's all the reaction I get from him, but for Jax that's telling enough. Well, he is oddly in a good mood today. I figured he'd be annoyed by now just sitting around babysitting me. He doesn't seem like the type to do well just sitting around.

Lindsey finally speaks up. I kind of forgot he was even in the room.

"Good to see that you are doing alright Percy. Eddy is going to be here to set up your new security equipment. He will be coming in and out but otherwise shouldn't bother you. I just came by to drop him off and to check in with Jaxson. Paxton will be coming with me to check on a few leads and Jaxson will be staying with you today and will switch out with either Paxton or I later. I will let you know if anything comes up, but so far, we are still just in the research phase. Nothing telling has shown up yet. Hopefully we will have more to go off with these leads we are running down. These guys know how to cover their tracks."

As he is finishing up his spiel Daphne comes bursting through the doors. "Percy! Did you know some random dude is dancing on our roof?!" She stops mid step when she finally looks up and sees the guys.

"Jesus Christ. More security guys and good god is it a requirement to be an Adonis to be part of this security team. Because I swear you all could be models if you get tired of private security."

Paxton laughs. He has met Daphne before, so he is kind of used to her. Jaxson's smile quirks just a little, but Lindsey just stares dumbstruck at her. Which makes me laugh. I didn't think anything would catch him off guard. He is always so stern and uptight. It seems that Daphne has made the big boss speechless. That doesn't surprise me though. She pretty much lights a room when she walks in. She is one of those people that are impossible to ignore.

"Hey Daph, the random guy is Eddy. He's the tech guy at Olympus Security and he's putting in a security system. He will be in and out today. Just ignore him. You know Pax and Jax, this is the big boss, Lindsey. He runs things." I wave my hand in Lindsey's direction even though he is a hard guy to miss. He's almost as big as Jaxson.

He finally steps up and puts his hand out to introduce himself. He tried to cover the awkwardness by clearing his throat. Which makes me giggle again. "Hello Daphne, I'm Lindsey. Please excuse my guys. They don't know how to act sometimes. Nice to put a face to the name finally. I've just read your name in my reports."

That makes Daphne stand a little straighter. "You have a dossier on me? Oh, how scandalous! I feel like I am in a Bond movie." I facepalm, Paxton chokes on a laugh, Jax doesn't move, and Lindsey again is speechless.

"Ooook. Well You guys have things to do so shoo and get on with all the spy things it is you do." I start to herd them out the door. "What are you doing here in the middle of the day Daphne? You usually aren't home till much later."

She doesn't say anything as she watches Pax and Lindsey walk out the door grudgingly. Finally, when they are no longer visible, she turns back to me,

"Huh? Oh right. I just came back to get a change of clothes. Nyx has a last-minute engagement tonight. I need a formal dress. So, I came back to get a few things to replenish my wardrobe that's in my office. I won't be here long. She has me running crazy to get things set up and move her schedule around. It's annoying. You know I hate last minute anything. I am good at my job because I am a planner. To the last detail. Being able to plan on the fly is part of the job, I know, I just don't like that part. And with her, I must look nice, but I can't upstage her."

She rolls her eyes as she's walking into her room mumbling about damn insecure women. It makes me chuckle. Daphne is effortlessly beautiful. She must actively work to tone it down to not "upstage" anyone. It still surprises me how we ended up so close. We are total opposites.

I shrug to myself and turn to look at Jaxson. We are the only two left in the room now. "What are the plans for the day?" He just stares at me for a moment, almost unblinking. I look pointedly at him and cross my arms. Two can play this game. I will stand here until he answers me. I have a feeling this could go on all day. I can be stubborn when I want to be.

Surprisingly, he gives up first. He drops his arms and sighs. "What do you have in mind?" He grumbles at me. It makes me a little giddy thinking about pushing this man to his boundaries. I feel like he has not had many people in his life who don't automatically back down from him. I think I am going to do everything I can to poke the bear. He can use a little loosening up and someone to keep him on his toes, and I need some amusement.

"I need to go to the job site and look around, to get a better idea of what I am working with and what angle I want to approach the case with. I haven't gone over there yet."

Before I even finish my sentence he immediately bristles back up. "No. Absolutely not." He shakes his head curtly for emphasis. "Not happening."

"What do you mean no? How do you expect me to work this case? I can't possibly fight for something when I don't have all the facts. I am still trying to win this case, you know. I can't do that half blind. I told you I intend to still win. That means I go about this the same way I always do. What's the big deal?"

"Big deal? We still do not have enough information on these guys. There has been no response, no follow-up after their initial threat. There is no way that they have just given up. They are biding their time for a reason. They have something up their sleeve, and until we know what that is you need to stay put and not go looking for trouble."

"I am not looking for trouble. Lindsey told me to go about my daily life and that is exactly what I plan on doing. Isn't that why you are here?" This has turned into a staring contest. I'm pretty sure I hear him mumbling about a stubborn woman, but I don't think too much of it because I see him moving towards the door and I think I won.

Chapter 12

Jaxson gave in and let me take my car. I think the only reason he did is because he was afraid of what I would do to his giant SUV, and he seemed to have paperwork or something to do. He's been pounding away on a laptop since we got in the car as usual. I am pretty used to his silence, so it doesn't bother me. I just hum away and dance to the music blaring through my speakers like he isn't even there. I am pretty content with my small victory so I can't keep the small smile off my face.

It takes about 30 minutes after the edge of town to get to the plot of land that I am researching. Well, the plot is kind of misleading. It's a lot of land. 500 acres of undisturbed Earth. I get out of the car and take a big deep breath. This is my favorite part of my job. I love it when I get to save some land that has yet to be touched. It's few and far between though. There isn't much around anymore that hasn't been touched in some way, shape, or form.

I pull my notes out to see what research I have so far. I am very curious to see how this place has managed to be safe so far. As I am glancing through my notes, wandering around aimlessly, I see out of the corner of my eye Jaxson has his gun out and is slightly crouched over. This puts me on high alert.

"What's going on? Did you see something? Are we not alone?"

My heart is pounding in my chest. He straightens back up.

"I thought I heard something, but I didn't see anything. I think I am just being on high alert because I feel like we are sitting ducks out here. You need to hurry up and get what you need so we can get the hell out of here. I am having a bad feeling. That is never a good thing."

I huff out a breath for him scaring the shit out of me for nothing. He is probably just being overly protective as usual.

I put my notes up back in my backpack and pulled out my camera. I can go over the history of this place more in depth later. I need to get as many pictures of this place as necessary to get a better idea of what I am working with. I am hoping I can find something unique in this property to make it easier for me to save.

I am sweaty from traipsing around in the woods for several hours taking pictures. I was trying to get every nest, every sighting of wildlife I could to use that as a possible angle. Jax has been following behind me silently, to his credit he hasn't complained once, but he still has his gun out. That is all the urging I need.

"Ok, I think that is all I need for now. We can head back so I can upload all these photos and comb through them in depth." I say to Jaxson over my shoulder while making my way towards my car. I'm pretty sure I hear him mumble "Thank Fuck" and that puts a smirk on my face.

"See, nothing happened. You were all uptight for nothing. You need to relax."

He grunts, "When I relax in my line of work, people die." Well ok then.

As I am throwing all my stuff into the backseat of my car, Jaxson opens a bottle of water and chugs half of it before he silently hands it over to me. As I am finishing it, he gets back into the passenger seat and gets his laptop back out.

WE HAVEN'T BEEN ON the road for too long before I start getting a bad feeling. I think that Jax's paranoia is rubbing off on me. I shake my head and roll my shoulders to try to shake the heebie jeebies away. I take a deep breath. Everything is fine, nothing is happening.

In the middle of my internal pep talk I glance up at my rearview mirror. There is a big SUV slowly trailing behind us. I normally would think nothing of it, but it looks exactly like the ones that all the boys drive in Olympus. The windows look too dark to not be just a little suspicious. I can't see the driver though because he is too far behind me.

I tap my brakes and slow down a little and notice that the SUV does the same. That's not good. They are too far behind me to have to worry about rear-ending me. The hair on my arms stands up. Uh oh. Looks like Jaxson's bad vibe may be onto something. Shit.

"Uh Jax." He must have heard something in my voice because he immediately came to attention and shuts his laptop. "What. What is it?" He snaps at me.

"So, you know how you were having a bad feeling? Well, I think that we are being followed." I whisper like the people in the car behind us can hear me. Don't judge, I've never been in a situation where I am legitimately scared for my life.

Jaxson takes one look behind us and says "Fuck! I knew this was a bad idea. I don't know how you manage to talk me out of my good sense." He looks around and points to the right. "There! Take that road. I need to see if they are really following us."

I whip my FJ Cruiser to the right, and sure enough thirty seconds later I see the black SUV turn behind me. Oh damn. This is not going to be good. I am resolutely trying not to panic as Jaxson whips his phone out. "Eddy! We have a possible situation. I need you to track our location. We have a tail. I don't know. I suspect the same. Yes! Get on it now!" He unceremoniously tosses his laptop in the back seat.

"Ok. Persephone. Relax. Take a deep breath."

I do as he says.

"Good. We have no idea if they are just tracking us or if they plan to engage. We need to try and lose them. Which is going to be difficult since we are in the middle of bumfucking nowhere."

He yanks at his hair in frustration. I glance at him quickly without turning my head. I am afraid if I look away for even a second, something crazy is going to happen.

I nod once. "Ok. Alright. It's fine. I'll just get to town the quickest way I can." I stepped on the gas a little. He touches my arm gently. "It's ok, Kitten. No matter what happens. I will not let anything happen to you. I promise. Do not go straight home. I am sure they already know where you live, but just in case we are not going to make it easy for them. Just keep doing what you are doing and stay as calm as possible. The last thing we need is to make it easy for them and you kill us in the car on the way home." He winks at me.

In the back of my mind, I know he is just trying to keep me calm, but the wink is so out of character for him my jaw drops open. He was successful at distracting me though. I'm too busy thinking about how that wink and smirk is going to play into my own personal fantasies later that I don't notice that the SUV has slammed on the gas and is rapidly approaching.

"Fuck! Ok, no matter what happens. You do NOT let them get to you, do you understand me? Do not let them get their hands on you. I don't care what you have to do to get away. You need to let all your pacifism go. You fight hard, and you fight dirty. This is about to get ugly but trust me. Trust that I'm going to do everything in my power to keep you safe."

He starts checking his seatbelt and mine to make sure that they are secure. At this moment I am kind of glad that I did not give in to my extreme conservation urges and get the tiny little smart car I was originally going to get. It's great on gas mileage, but I am pretty sure that we are about to get rammed, and my FJ Cruiser won't crumple like a toy car at least.

My heart is beating frantically, and I am only able to take shallow breaths. I'm on the verge of having a panic attack. "Kitten! Listen to me!" Jaxson barks at me. "You cannot panic. We are going to get through this. We knew that they were going to eventually take a shot at you, and we are prepared." He starts pulling his gun back out.

Oh god, oh shit. Shit. Shit. Shit. I just keep mumbling shit over and over. When I looked up the SUV is right behind us. "Oh God! Jaxson! What do I do! I have never had to out drive someone before. I don't know what the hell to do! There's nowhere to go!"

He is frantically looking around, but he was right. We are in the middle of nowhere. Damn it! Why didn't I listen to him? Stupid! Nothing had happened so I thought they were being paranoid. I guess I should have listened to them. They do know what they are talking about. They do this for a living. I guess this is what Russo wanted. Stay back and stay quiet until I got overly confident and did something stupid. Fucking mobsters.

Chapter 13

I can now hear the revving of the engine behind me, and I brace for the hit that I know is coming. Right as I had thought, my car jerks from the impact. My tires squeal and I am pretty sure so do I. I try swerving over to the other lane to get away from them and stomp on the gas, but their tank has much more horsepower than I do.

"Hang on!" Jaxson yells. He is rolling his window down and trying to maneuver himself out the window with his gun. Jesus Christ this is like a scene from a freaking action movie! How did this become my life?

I hear shots being fired. I am in too much of a panic to know if they are coming from Jaxson or if they are coming at him. I am too busy trying to keep my car from rolling with the continuous impacts hitting me from behind to be able to distinguish anything else.

I yell. "I don't think that we can do this much longer! My car isn't meant to be part of a demolition derby!" Jaxson gets back in the window. "I know. Just do your best to keep us upright but prepare yourself for the worst."

Worst? What's the worst? We are already being slammed into and being shot at. What could be much worse? Then I see the road narrow. Really Universe! You just had to see what you could do, didn't you? I shouldn't have opened my mouth. Or thoughts. Whatever. I'm rambling to myself.

My tires are squealing as I take a turn too quickly, and one last tap from the SUV behind me was finally enough. I can feel us tipping as my car loses control. It all happens so fast, yet in slow motion at the same time.

I let go of the wheel and look over at Jaxson as we start to roll. My heart stops beating for a moment. The lines of his jaw are sharp from the tension of these circumstances. We are in a really shitty situation that neither one of us knows how it's going to end but knowing that it's going to end badly. Are we going to survive this? Maybe. I doubt I'll come out of this whole though. This split second of letting go of the wheel is a pivotal moment. The shit is about to hit the fan and rain down on us. What the hell do I do now?

With each impact of my car rolling, my head is being slammed around and Jaxson is doing his best to keep himself from going out the window. He never put his seatbelt back on when he was done hanging out of the car in the middle of his little shootout. He's holding on for dear life, because if he lets that go, it most certainly will be the end of his.

It's strange the things that you notice when you are in the middle of a car accident. The smell of the rubber from the tires burning out. The look of Jaxson's muscles bulging underneath his t-shirt while he is holding onto the oh shit handle. The feel of the tiny cuts on your skin from glass shattering. It's a very surreal moment.

I must have blacked out for a minute because when I have my next conscious thought, I am hanging upside down and feel someone trying to drag me out of my smashed window. I managed to release my seatbelt and smack into the floor, well roof, of my car and grunt with the pain. Everything hurts, and blood is running down my face.

I don't really have time to think much about it though. Whoever is trying to get me is still trying to grab my kicking legs. I try to shake Jaxson who is still unconscious in the seat next to me. Despite my best efforts of kicking the shit out of whoever is grabbing me, he still manages to get a secure grip on me and starts dragging me outside of the car.

"JAXSON! Jaxson wake up! Help me!"

I am screaming at him, hoping to God he wakes up in time and I don't get taken. I took Krav Maga classes the entire time I was in college. I didn't want to leave myself completely vulnerable, being a single chick in the city, but I have never actually had to use it on someone. I'm pretty sure these guys are professional henchmen too and I doubt all the time I spent on all those self defense classes are going to do me any good, but Jaxson said fight dirty. I will fight with everything I have too. I highly doubt anything good will come of them kidnapping me. Considering they want me dead and all.

I am kicking and screaming and hitting everything that I can touch trying to make it as difficult as possible for this dude. He is big. Not near as big as Jaxson is, and not as fit, but he is still huge compared to me. That's not really a hard thing to accomplish though. I'm short, but I am in shape now, and I will use that to my advantage. I notice on his neck is that weird peace sign symbol, so I am without a doubt now that this is one of Russo's guys.

I am rapidly going through all my self defense training I can think of in the middle of my panic. I managed to kick him in the balls, and he drops my foot. I am scratched all to hell, bleeding in multiple places, pretty sure I have a concussion, but none of that matters right now. I am officially in fight or flight mode. I have adrenaline pumping through me, so when he drops my foot, I immediately start running.

I slide around Jaxson's side of the car to try to get him to wake up and help me, but he is already dragging himself out of the car.

"Shit! Jax get moving! This bastard is trying to get me!"

My screaming puts him into high gear, and he stands up and throws himself into the guy who is trying to grab me again and tackles him. I am huddling by the side of the car trying to get my breathing under control as I am listening to the sounds of fists pummeling into each other. It's a sickening sound.

While I am trying to not have a panic attack, I hear Jaxson yell for me.

"Percy!"

He grunts from what I assume a fist to his middle.

"Find my gun!"

The car is a mess. It's smashed all up with glass and everything that was inside strewn all over the pavement. I crawl inside and frantically start throwing everything to the side looking for Jaxson's gun. I keep hearing the men pounding into each other and I don't know how much more Jax can take. He is already beaten up from the accident.

What seems like forever, but is probably only a couple of minutes, I finally feel the cold steel of the gun on my fingertips. Thank fuck! I grabbed it and started sliding back out of the car to get it to Jaxson as quickly as possible.

Is he expecting me to use it? I hope not. I have held a gun before, I am from the south after all, but I have never shot at anything but clay pigeons before. So, I don't think me having it is going to do us much good. I may have shot Jaxson by accident.

"Jaxson! I've got it!"

He takes a second to look over at me and it costs him getting a fist to the face. He barely even flinches as he uses all this weight to shove the guy off him so he can take a step towards me to get the gun.

The second he has it in his hand he whips around just as the henchman is leaping towards him. Jaxson gets a couple shots off to his chest right before the henchman's body slams into him. The impact knocks him backwards and he lands on the ground with the guy's body on top of him, but his shots must have been true because the guy isn't moving.

My ass hits the pavement as it gets quiet and the adrenaline pumping through me leaves as fast as it came. I can suddenly feel all my cuts and bruises. Jaxson rolls the body off of him and gets to his feet. He wobbles a little as he stands up. It just takes him a couple steps to get to me and he drops to his knees as he grabs my face. "Percy. Are you ok? Are you seriously hurt? Talk to me!" I grab ahold of his forearms like they are a lifeline while I am trying to get my breathing under control enough to answer him, but I look over and see the body.

I Seeing a man lying on the pavement in the middle of all the wreckage with a pool of blood expanding around him makes me start to panic again.

"He's dead. We killed a man."

I'm shaking so hard that I am pretty sure it's making Jaxson shake too with him holding on to me.

"I killed a man. Not you. Don't look at him. It's ok now. You're safe. I've got you. Just take a deep breath."

I nod a couple times as I start taking deep breaths. Jaxson pulls his phone out of his pocket. I have no idea how the hell it managed to stay in there while we were rolling down an embankment.

"Yes. We're fine. I need a clean up crew and transportation. Our vehicle is shot to shit. Send someone to come get us. She's fine, a little banged up, but she's tough. She will be alright."

Tough? I don't feel very tough right now.

Jaxson sits down next to me and pulls me to him.

"You did so good. You did exactly like I told you to, and you fought. I am very proud of you; you didn't let your panic throw you into shock. If you hadn't kept it together while I was unconscious, he would have gotten you."

"Well, I was really lucky there was only one of them. If there had been more, I would have been fucked. Probably literally too." I take a shaky breath. "I'm sorry I didn't listen to you. This wouldn't have happened if I just would have stayed my ass at home!"

"If it wasn't today, it was going to happen eventually. We were lucky. Lindsey is sending people to come help. Just hang tight."

Chapter 14

We got dropped back off at the house after Jaxson's people showed up and gave us a car. I am still kind of in a daze, so I don't even really remember him putting me in the car, or the drive home. I just have the last couple hours on a rapid reel going through my mind.

Despite the threats, I never actually thought that my life was in danger. I honestly believed that they were just that, threats. Not anymore. My small delusions have now been shattered to a thousand pieces. Someone is trying to kill me. If it wasn't for Jaxson, they would have succeeded. He saved my life. I don't even know how to feel about that right now. I feel broken. I'm covered in dirt, grime, and blood. Oh god that man's blood is on me. He's dead. I have never seen someone die in person before. Movies do not do it justice. It's brutal and messy. The sounds, the smells, it is all something that I don't think I am going to be able to get out of my head for a long time.

I can't imagine that Giuseppe Russo is going to be very happy to find out that his henchman is dead, and I am not. I can't think about that right now though. I can't stop shaking and I feel numb. I need to shower. I need to get this filth off me, but I am just standing here in the middle of the bathroom with the water running and not moving. I know that I must be in shock. I mean, who wouldn't be in this situation. I am not a crime fighter. I am a environmentalist for Christ's sake! I don't deal with death and mayhem. I don't even like confrontation, and now I am in the midst of one giant clusterfuck of a confrontation and not sure how I got here.

This whole situation is traumatizing, but I can't be weak. If I let myself shut down, I can end up being killed. Not to mention, if the boys see me breaking down then they are going to coddle me. I definitely don't want to be the helpless female that constantly needs rescued and reassured. Ugh. This is crazy. Get it together Percy!

I start to mechanically take off my tattered clothes. My hands are shaking so bad it makes the buttons difficult. I finally got undressed and get under the scalding hot water. Maybe I can burn the images from my brain.

The wreckage. My poor car. The feeling of tumbling for what felt like hours before we slammed into the ditch. The sounds of the pounding of fists into flesh when Jaxson was fighting for our lives. I shudder. I need to let it go. Dwelling on these issues isn't going to help. But I can't. A sob shakes loose. I slide down the walls of the shower and lift my knees to my chest as the tears start falling. I'm now shaking harder from the sobs that are wrecking through my chest. My tiny bubble of contentment has just popped.

I am usually great at finding the silver lining in any situation. I am a glass half full kind of girl, but this time I am coming up empty. I want to yell to the Universe. Why? Why is this happening to me? I've dedicated my life to doing good. I am a good person. Why is this shitty situation happening to me? What did I do to deserve this?

I look up when I hear the shower door slide open. It's Jaxson. If I wasn't in such a state of shock already, I most definitely would be now. Jaxson steps into the shower bare chested but still wearing his jeans. He walks under the spray and lifts me to his chest. He must have heard me crying, or maybe he just instinctively knew that I needed someone. It takes me off guard for a second. He is normally so reserved and doesn't ever touch me. So the fact that he is holding me is surprising. I don't know how to respond to this softer side of him, but when he wraps his arms around me and holds me tightly to his chest I don't care. Another sob breaks through.

"SShh. It's ok. I've got you."

Jaxson murmurs into my hair. That makes me cry harder. I'm not comfortable with the fact that his life was on the line to save mine. I know that it's his job, but I am not sure I can accept the cost.

"I can't. I can't let you. You had to kill a man for me!"

I choke on the word kill.

"Don't worry about that right now. I've done worse. Turn around."

He gently turns my back to him, and I hear a lid pop. The revelation that he is washing me quiets my sobs down to sniffles. I stay quiet. I don't want to ruin this moment. I can't imagine that Jaxson makes any kind of gestures lightly, so I stand still while he methodically washes and rinses my hair and begins to wash my body. I should be embarrassed. We have never been on this level of comfort with each other, and he sure as hell has never seen me naked, but I can't bring myself to care.

I watch as the grime slides down the drain. He's touching me like I am going to break, maybe I will. I feel like this behemoth of a man touching me so softly, like I'm fragile, is going to make me shatter into a million pieces. He finishes washing all the dirt away and turns me back towards him.

"You just went through a very traumatizing event. It's ok to be upset. It's ok to need a moment. I would be worried if you didn't. I'm here to help you through it. If you break, I'm here to put you back together. Take a minute. No one will see you as weak for this."

It's scary how well he reads me. He steps out of the shower and grabs a towel and holds it out for me to step into. Not caring that he is still wearing jeans that are soaking wet and hanging dangerously low on his hips. "Take all the time that you need. I'll be in the kitchen when you are ready." With that, he walks out the door to give me a second to get my shit together.

Now that I am breathing just a little easier, I hear arguing. The rest of the boys must have heard what happened and are here. I take a deep breath and leave the safety of the bathroom to get dressed and see what's going on.

Chapter 15

I step into the kitchen, and it takes a moment for anyone to even realize that I am standing there. Jaxson is standing ramrod straight with his fists clenched to his side while Paxton is in his face yelling. It catches me off guard. Paxton is always happy go lucky. I have never heard him raise his voice before, but there he is. Red faced and a vein popping out on the side of his neck yelling at Jaxson.

"What the fuck were you thinking? She could have fucking died. DIED. She got fucking lucky, because I have no god damned idea how she managed to get away from one of Russo's men all on her own! Alone! Where the fuck were you when she was being dragged across the goddamn pavement! I can only imagine what she looks like right now!"

Jaxson interrupts his tirade by shoving his hands into Paxton's chest and knocking him back a couple steps.

"You don't think I fucking know this?! I was there Pax! I was next to her trembling. Terrified out of her mind when reality hit. I was there when I saw the look on her face when the car started to roll. I was there when I could see how she looked at me after I beat and shot a man to death with my bare hands in front of her!" Jaxson rakes his hands through his hair like he is trying to pull it out by the roots. He says, "I was fucking there" barely above a whisper. If I wasn't staring at him so intently, I would have missed it.

He looks so disheveled. He changed into some sweats, but he is still shirtless with bare feet, like Paxton showed up in the middle of his dressing. I am momentarily sidetracked by his feet. It's so out of place. I don't ever see Jaxson relaxed enough like that. Who would have thought feet could be sexy?

I'm snapped out of my ogling by Lindsey's voice. He steps up in between Pax and Jax with his arms outstretched to the side, keeping them apart. I am sure, with all these testosterone filled men, this is not the first time he has had to break someone up close to coming to blows.

"Guys! This is not going to do any good. I know everyone's emotions are running high right now. None of us are happy that Percy got hurt, but now is not the time to fight over who is to blame. We need to get our shit together fast. Only as a team are we going to be able to protect her and make sure that this does not happen again. She may not be so lucky next time." He looks over to Paxton. "And you need to back off. It could have easily been you out there. Jaxson did the best he could with the situation he was given. She may be a little banged up, but she's ok Pax."

Paxton's chest is heaving like he just ran a mile. Jaxson is staring at the ground not moving a muscle, looking like he is lost. I don't like this look on him. I don't know why he is beating himself up over this. He did protect me. He saved me. He killed a man for me.

I take another step into the kitchen to interfere. It is not ok for Paxton to be taking his frustration out on Jax like he did something wrong. That man has saved more than my physical body today. He picked up all my broken pieces and shoved them back together when I was losing myself and unable to breathe. I don't know if he has succeeded. I still feel like I am frayed at the edges, but I do know that if he hadn't come into that shower, I would still be sitting there in shock instead of standing right now.

All their heads whip in my direction when I finally speak up.

"Paxton, you are not being fair to him. It was my fault that we were even out there to begin with. I convinced him to let me go. I wouldn't be standing here right now if it wasn't for Jaxson. He saved my life."

My voice tapered off at the end. To my credit it didn't break. I have been able to keep in the tears pushing at the back of my eyes. I don't want them to think I am weak. I don't want them to see me broken. They must still be able to see it though. Lindsey is giving me a look of pity. Paxton jumps in my direction like he's going to grab me. It makes me flinch. He sees it and stops immediately.

"Shit Percy. I wasn't going to hurt you." Paxton says with a look of hurt on his face.

"I know. I'm sorry. I can't help it. I guess I'm still shaken up a bit."

I look down at my feet from embarrassment. I'm sure my cheeks are flaming red right now. I didn't mean to flinch. I mean, it's Paxton for god's sake. I know he would never hurt me, but I can't help still being a little raw after almost being abducted. It's going to take a minute for me to not jump at a man trying to put his hands on me in any way.

Seeing the look of pure evil on that man's face while he was trying to drag me through my broken car window flashes through my mind. I shake my head to try to dispel those images. Now is not the time to break down again.

Immediately I feel a finger lifting my chin up. Jaxson is looking me in the eyes.

"Do not apologize. You have every right to be uneasy right now. No one expects you to be unaffected by all this. Are you ok?" I try to speak, but I am afraid I will start crying again if I do, so I just nod. He takes a step back.

When I look back up, Paxton is looking at Jax weirdly and Lindsey is standing there with the corners of his mouth twitching. Like he knows a secret. Paxton takes a step closer to me with his hands up where I can see them.

"I just want to get a look at you Darlin'. You scared the shit out of me. When Boss called me and told me what happened I didn't know what I was going to be coming here to."

He uses his index finger to move my face side to side.

"Shit Darlin' You scratched your pretty face all up."

He looks me up and down. It makes me slightly uncomfortable, and I start to fidget.

"Well,", he sighs "it could have been a lot worse. I am surprised how good you look after seeing the scene of the accident. Your car was smashed to hell."

The reminder of my car being totaled makes me sniff. I loved that car. Panda must sense my distress because she comes running out of her house and climbs up my pants and holds onto my neck like she is trying to comfort me.

"Hey Panda. I was wondering where you were. Did these big bad men screaming at each other scare you?" I nuzzled my face into her fur and kiss her face.

She gets annoyed by my cuddling and immediately jumps down and runs towards the kitchen. This makes me chuckle. At least she took a second away from looking for food to check on me. Paxton is shaking his head at me.

I raised an eyebrow at him. "What?" He chuckles. "I still can't believe you have a damn raccoon as a pet."

This makes me put my hands on my hips and square off with him.

"Why? You have a problem with Panda?"

I am angry glaring at him now. He can say all he wants about me, but Panda is an amazing pet. He better not say shit about her. I may be a pacifist normally, but I will fight for what I love. Panda has been a constant in my life for years. Yes, it's a little weird I ended up with a trash panda as a pet and not a dog like normal people, but I have never really been normal anyway. I am totally fine with being the weird one, it works for me. My emotions are just shredded enough to be in defense mode instantly.

"Woah. Hey now. I ain't saying nothing about Miss Panda." He looks over at Jaxson, "Damn if looks could kill I'd be dead right now.

I thought she was all make love and not war and shit." That makes everyone laugh and breaks the tension.

"Sorry Pax. I'm just a little one edge. I need some coffee." I take a step towards the kitchen, but Jaxson puts a hand on my shoulder.

"Go sit down. I'll get you some coffee."

Huh. Coffee delivered. I could get used to this. Though, I would not like to have a repeat moment of my almost dying just for coffee. Well, ok coffee is life, and I may second guess for just a minute over it.

Paxton and Lindsey followed me over to the living room. Oh man. We're about to talk about all this. I really don't want to rehash the chaos. I am already going to obsess over every minor detail all on my own when I get a second to breathe.

Quite frankly I would rather try to forget all about it and never think of it again. Lindsey is giving me a sympathetic look like he knows what I'm thinking. Maybe he saw me grimace. I wouldn't doubt it. I am terrible at hiding things. Everything shows on my face. That's the main reason why I don't lie. Besides morals and all that, it's useless because my facial expressions give me away every time.

I am momentarily distracted from my mental rambling by watching Paxton try to sit on one of the bean bags. He plops down on it, but his arms start flailing while he is trying to get situated. He ends up sliding all the way off the other side and slams into the floor with an ummph.

"God damn it! Why the hell do you even have these things! Normal people have things called chairs."

His grumbling to himself as he is trying to wrestle himself into a comfortable position on the bean bag makes me crack up laughing.

I am laughing so hard that tears are streaming down my face. I have no idea why I am laughing so hard because it wasn't that funny. My emotions are all over the damn place right now. I am sure I look completely crazy. It's just the vision of seeing a man over six feet tall, packed with muscle, sliding around on a bean bag chair is hilarious.

They are large bean bag chairs made for adults, so it's not my fault he's so damn big he doesn't fit on them.

He is flinging his legs out, trying to cross one on over his other knee, trying to sit Indian style, unable to get comfortable.

"How the hell are you even supposed to sit on these things?"

He flails his arms back out again trying to keep from falling off again. Lindsey is looking at him horrified. I end up bending over, half gasping for breath trying to calm myself as Jaxson sets a cup of coffee down on the table next to me.

Before he ends up sitting down next to me, he walks over and smacks Paxton on the back of his head.

"Get your shit together man. It's embarrassing." This starts my giggling all over again.

Chapter 16

Things have pretty much gone back to normal. We are back to the usual routine of the guys taking turns guarding me and following my every move. Though nothing else has happened in a while, I have still avoided going anywhere besides work and home. I haven't even ventured out to the gym. I am still terrified that someone is watching me and just waiting to jump at the opportunity to try and grab me again.

I am at work today with Paxton. He has come with me enough times now that everyone in the office is used to him being there. He usually spends the day making the rounds and harassing whoever he can to keep himself occupied. It's common to hear lots of laughter these days. It usually makes me shake my head and smile, but I don't have it in me today. You can't help but love Pax. He is so lighthearted and does what he can to put a smile on people's faces, no matter how ridiculous he must be.

I am watching him terrorize poor Katie at the front desk. She is embarrassed super easily, so Paxton's incessant flirting makes her face turn as red as a tomato. I think he does it just to see how red he can make her get, like it's his own personal game. Normally this would make me giggle, but I have been in a funk lately. I can't seem to shake the feeling of being desperate and under attack. It's not knowing what's coming next that gets you.

You know it's not the end, something is still out there, but you have no idea what it is and when it's happening. The saying "the suspense is killing me" is a very real thing. It makes you feel like your body is in a constant fight or flight situation and it's exhausting.

You would think being in the environmental field and seeing how little people care, how selfish humans are in general, would make me cynical. It hasn't though. Even though I see everyday how thoughtless and destructive people are, I have been able to maintain the idea that people are generally good.

I don't really know how to feel right now though. I want to be angry, occasionally I want to retaliate, but it's not in my general nature. My emotions are all over the place and it's making me edgy and not like myself. The weight of my oscillating feelings is suffocating, but I also don't know how to get out from under it either. They don't teach you how to let go of the threat of death when they teach you how to meditate.

We haven't seen hide nor hair of any of Russo's people lately. It doesn't make me feel better though. In fact, it makes me more nervous. Like I am in the calm before the storm. Just sitting around waiting for the boogieman to jump out of the shadows.

Which is an apt description of Giuseppe Russo. The boogie man. He stays in the shadows, just lurking outside your field of sight, making the hair on your arm stand on end. You know he's there, but you never see him until you are at your most vulnerable and he can drag you into the inky blackness of the dark. Leaving you unable to tell up from down and utterly terrified.

Ugh! I hate that man. He is a vile human being, and the fact that he is pulling this negativity out of me makes me hate him even more. I have never even done anything to slight him, didn't even know of his existence until now, but that doesn't matter. When he wants something, he takes it. Without thought, or without conscience, he will do whatever he has to to get what he wants.

Right now, he wants something that I am in the way of, and I am not backing down. Sorry Russo. You terrify me, but I am not letting this go. I will do whatever I can to make sure you don't win this time. They say nice guys finish last, but I am not feeling very nice right now. Now I am just pissed off.

I must have been staring off into space and thinking hard because my cell phone vibrates next to me and makes me jump. I am still not used to anyone calling or texting me. The only person I normally ever hear from is Daphne, but all the boys have my number now and text me pretty frequently. I look down to see who it is. Paxton is usually the one blowing up my phone, sending me a bunch of random memes or gifs, but he is with me so it can't be him.

JAXSON: KITTEN

Persephone: Yes?

Hmm. It's Jaxson. I wonder if something has happened. He isn't much for idle chit chat. Usually if he is messaging me, he is relaying some sort of information, checking on schedules, or letting me know any changes. He has always been a man of few words, but he has been more open lately. Maybe he's just worried that I am going to fall apart again, since he was the only one to see me break down.

Jaxson: You at work?

Persephone: Uh, you make my schedule. I am pretty sure that you know that I am. What's up? Did something happen?

Jaxson: No. There is nothing new to report. I am just checking on you. Making sure you are alright.

Persephone: I'm fine Jaxson. Paxton is with me. I haven't gone anywhere or done anything that you don't know about. I'm staying in my box like a good little girl and doing what I am told.

Ok, so maybe I'm a little bitter, but don't judge me. It's hard going from being alone all the time, not having to answer to anyone but yourself, to having your every move watched. Now I am never alone. I know they mean well. They are just looking out for me. They are being paid to look out for me. Damn. The only people who are looking out for my wellbeing right now are being paid to do so. Wow. That's sad. Now I am definitely feeling bitter.

Jaxson: You know we are just trying to keep you safe.

I just lay my phone down and don't even answer him. I have heard this excuse so many times lately. It's their answer to everything. I get it. I appreciate all that they are doing for me, but damn I am tired of them sounding like a broken record!

I ignore the buzz because I have nothing to say right now that isn't going to make me sound like a total bitch. I know it's not his fault, but I just don't care right now. I don't care if it's out of character, or unlike me. My complete focus is on putting together the strongest case I can and sticking it to Mr. Russo. He. Will. Not. Win.

The court date is coming up very soon to present our case to the judge, and I am going to make damn sure that we keep our winning streak and that we do not lose this one. I may not be able to stand against Russo on the streets, but I can stand against him in a courtroom, well metaphorically. I won't be the one physically standing in front of him in a courtroom. Just my words, my information, and my plan of action. Good luck Giuseppe Russo, hope you have a lawyer who can outsmart me. You'll be in my world now.

Chapter 17

Today is the day of the preliminary hearing. My nerves are already shot to hell. I have already drunk one cup of coffee and on my second one while I stared listlessly into my closet trying to decide what to wear.

Paxton walks into my room, "Darlin' calm down. I can feel your nerves from the living room."

I give him a dry look.

"Haven't you ever heard that the worst thing that you can tell an upset woman is to calm down. It's never a good idea. That will do you about as much good as throwing a shoe at a hornet's nest."

I turn back around to peruse my closet. Looking back over my shoulder I continue my gentle reprimand, "lucky for you, I am not mad. Just nervous. Now actually make yourself useful and help me figure out what to wear."

Paxton chuckles while rubbing his hands together. "Now that, I can help you with!" I did not like the glint in his eye. Maybe this was not a good idea.

"Respectable! It must be respectable. I am going to court after all." I yell at him as he ducks into my walk-in closet.

"Have faith Darlin'. Have faith!" I hear his muffled response as I drop my butt unceremoniously onto my bed while I wait to see how bad I am going to regret asking him for help.

Jaxson, Paxton, and Lindsey accompanied me to the courthouse. Which in my opinion, is a little overkill. I mean I know that Russo will be here in person, but what is he going to do in a packed courthouse.

Off me in front of a judge? Not likely. He has managed to keep himself from being incriminated so far in any of the other massive amount of cases they have tried to pin on him, so I highly doubt he will ruin that track record for me. It would be nice though. It would make my life a hell of a lot easier for sure. Alas, that is wishful thinking. As much as I think it's overkill, I really do appreciate the support though.

We walked in and sat in the back row, they sandwiched me in the middle of these three massive dudes and somehow found a shadow to throw me under as well. Cue mental eye roll now. I mildly huff as I unceremoniously plop myself down into my seat as I watch all the lawyers getting themselves prepared in the front of the courtroom.

I watch Carlton, the lawyer that is representing my firm in the case, roll his shoulders back and tilt his head side to side like he is getting ready for the boxing ring. Which I guess is appropriate when you are going up against the likes of Giuseppe Russo. I definitely do not envy him and really appreciate my relative anonymity right now.

I feel all the guys stiffen next to me as an eerie silence flow through the courtroom. I raise myself just a little bit higher in my seat to try to see what is going on up there. Being short has its serious disadvantages sometimes. As I am lifting my chin to get a better view, I feel a hand pressed down on my shoulders. Pushing hard enough to make me slam back down in my seat. I turn towards the man attached to said hand and put on my fiercest glower. "What the hell?" I hiss quietly at Jax. "I am just trying to see what's going on. Why did everyone go so silent? It gave me goosebumps like someone just saw a ghost." I raise my arm up to show him the hairs standing up on their ends. He gives me his usual grunt and nods his chin forward subtly. "Russo. That's why."

I quickly sink back down into my seat and slouch down as I see him scanning the courtroom. Oh shit. I hope he didn't see me. I slowly glance back up and feel, actually feel the ripples of revulsion flowing down my body, as I see him looking directly at me. His hard, cold stare makes my heart start pumping a million miles an hour.

Oh crap. Oooooh crap. This was a terrible idea. So so bad. Such a bad idea. Why did I come here? Why in the name of all that is holy did I think this was a good idea. If I didn't feel like I had a target on my back, I sure as hell do now. That was most definitely not a friendly look. That was the kind of look that I feel like Ted Bundy gave to the dog that he and Liz were looking into buying when it started growling at him. Side note: I am perversely into all things crime related. The only tv I ever really watched. Hence all the old school Mob references. I recently watched the documentary of Ted Bundy's trials since I have been spending so much time sequestered in my home. I have made a lot more use of Daph's tv than I ever have. Awesome movie by the way. You should watch it.

I'm nervous because my internal ramblings have gone off the deep end again. So sorry. I guess you should be used to it by now though. I tilt my head to the side as I look back up at him again. He is no longer looking at me, so I have a chance to study him a little more intensely. As I watch him smile genuinely and shake hands with the other attorneys, and then walk over to his opposing counsel and smile and shake hands with them as well, it strikes me that there are a lot of similarities to him and Bundy. Handsome, charming, personable, and brilliant. Though I would say that Russo takes the cake in the brains department because he has yet to be charged with anything.

My mind continues to ramble down this path as I have zoned out while the proceedings have begun. Being that this is just a preliminary hearing, they are not going to get too in depth with any information or anything. It's just the initial this is what I want and he can't have it and this is what I want and you should give it to me blah blah blahs. I know what our side is going to say because well I wrote it so, not necessary for me to stay too focused.

I did have every intention of listening to what Bundy's, I mean Russo's, side has to say about it to get more information on how to refute it, but sadly when I zone out, I zone out hard. Before I know it Jaxson is all but lifting me up out of my seat and beelining for the door.

"Uhhhh, is it already over?"

I huff between breaths as I am all but running to keep up with Jaxson and his hold on my arm. He looks down at me with a confused look on his face but doesn't say anything. He, on the other hand, is unilaterally focused on getting my ass out of dodge.

"Dude," I yank on my arm a little. "You are going to pull my arm out of its socket. I am way shorter than you, I can not keep up and that is starting to hurt."

He immediately slows down at that, but not by much. He is still rapidly weaving me in and out of people who are crammed into the front of the courthouse. Paxton is on my other side and Lindsey is walking behind me. Back to the part about being sandwiched between all this massive man meat. This could go a whole other way and be a lot more pleasant. I snort out loud at that thought process and Jaxson again looks down at me, but this time looking like I have lost my mind. Paxton is glancing over at me with a smirk on his face like he can read my mind. I very maturely stuck my tongue out at him.

This very brief interaction was apparently all the hesitation needed for a train wreck to occur. When I look back forward, and put my tongue back in my mouth, I feel all the guys stiffen again. Before I can even figure out why this time, I hear my name being all but yelled at me.

"Mrs. Walters." I immediately know who it is, and I stop dead in my tracks. Oh shit.

Chapter 18

I started looking around to try to find out where the sound of my name came from. It only takes a second for me to finally see him standing there not far in front of me. I am momentarily taken aback by the thought of how in the hell he made it out here so fast, and to end up in front of me.

The man without a face that has featured in my nightmares for months. The unseen force that has been literally a threat to my life, one that I have known in name only. It's suddenly more real, despite everything that has happened, this instant it has exploded into reality. I expected all kinds of things from him, but I am kind of taken aback by the reality. He's attractive. Of course, the bastard is. He is tall but not bulky. I would put money on the fact that there is nothing but lean muscle under that suit. I mean, the right-hand man of a mob boss is not going to be weak. His skin is the color of caramel, and his hair is jet black. He looks like a well to do businessman. You would never know there is anything behind that until you look at his eyes. They're hard and dark, like obsidian. Those are the eyes of a calculating mind, and he is walking right towards me.

I straighten my spine and hold my head up. Hoping to God that he doesn't notice the shake in my legs. He looks like a damn panther stalking his prey right now, but I refuse to show him just how much he terrifies me. I have heard and seen way too much from this man not to be nervous in his presence. He's the type of man that despises weakness but instills fear.

He walks right up to me and puts his hand out.

"Mrs. Walters. It's nice to finally meet you."

He has a smirk on his face that I want to smack off. He knows damn well there is nothing nice about this. I don't take his hand. He drops his and his smirk twitches like he is fighting to keep the amicable expression on his face.

"Mr. Russo, I presume." I raise an eyebrow at him wondering what the hell he is getting at. "How can I help you?"

His smile grows. "

Oh, Percy, they do call you Percy, right? There are many things that you can help me with, but I just came over to officially introduce myself."

He has a slight accent. Of course, he does. Can this get anymore cliche? Tall, dark, handsome, wearing an expensive suit, and with Italian leather shoes. I do a mental eye roll. I swear this guy thinks he is Al Capone.

"Only my friends call me Percy. Sorry, but that counts you out."

He makes a tsk noise like he is about to scold a child.

"Now, now. No need to be rude. We're just having a friendly chat. Getting to know each other."

That makes me huff out a laugh.

"Friendly? I don't think there is anything friendly about any kind of confrontation with you, and excuse me if I am not worried about my manners when it comes to someone who is trying to off me."

It's his turn to laugh. It's deep and low. Menacing. Not at all amusing.

"There is no proof of me doing anything quite so heinous. Though there have been many trying to prove otherwise and failed. I am simply going up against you in the court of law to win what should rightfully be mine. Legally and respectfully."

He takes a step closer to me.

"I find your... Fire...amusing. I am interested to see what is to come of our little encounter. Though, I would like it even more if you would simply concede and give me what I want."

I take a step back. It makes me bump into Jaxson. Paxton and he had been standing silently beside me, but Jaxson has now taken position at my back. Here for support but just watching what is happening. He is stiff and poised to take action if this gets ugly. Again, I don't think that anything is going to happen right now though. I think Guiseppe is just trying to scare me. It's too public of a place for him to do anything rash, especially with reporters milling about at the bottom of the courthouse stairs. Right now, he is wearing his public persona. He won't do anything to let anyone see him differently. That's why he has his flunkies do his dirty work for him.

Jaxson puts his hand subtly on my lower back to steady me. I appreciate his support. It makes me stand a little taller.

"I can see where people find you charming, but to me you are just condescending. If I haven't backed off the case already with your...associates... Sending your messages to me, don't think that I will now. I don't do veiled threats and mind games Sir. It's my job to protect what doesn't have a voice and can't do it on their own. I have never let anyone bully me into giving up, and I don't plan on doing so now. I have righteous anger and human decency on my side."

I swear his eyes got darker.

"Hm. It's cute how you look through rose colored glasses. Those who are moral and decent are not the ones who usually get anywhere in life. What is that saying? Nice guys finish last, yes? I think that is said for a reason. Those who are ruthlessly cunning and well off always win. I have both in spades. Good luck. It is not even about the land any longer. Now, I just want to watch you break when your self-righteous ideals shatter to pieces."

He turns around and walks off, leaving me speechless.

Paxton lets out a whistle, "Darlin' I think you just poked the bear."

Jaxson grabs ahold of my elbow and begins steering me towards the car. A little too forcefully again I might add. He growls at me. "You have just made yourself a challenge to him. He is going to up his game just to make a point now. You just couldn't keep your mouth shut, could you?"

I don't even know what to say to that because what just happened sinks in. Shit. I just poked the bear. I just threw down the gauntlet to a man that has never lost. A ruthless, brutal man that does not care to mow down anyone in his wake. I mentally smack my forehead.

Chapter 19

Since the initial court proceedings have started, I don't have much to do. I have finished all my research, mapped out how to present the evidence, and given my advice and opinions on how everything was going to go. I thought of every possible question, and rebuttal, that I could think of. I gave everything to the lawyers, and it is up to them now.

I found our ace in the hole. After scouring thousands of photos that I took over and over I finally found it. I was getting desperate and nervous that I wasn't going to be able to pull this one off. I had some back up plans that MAY have worked but I was really hoping that I would have a slam dunk case, and I found it. In the background of one of the photos I took was a tiny little plant. The untrained eye wouldn't even have recognized it. But since this is not just my job, but my passion, I spotted it right away.

What did I find? Lomatium Bradshawii, or Bradshaw's desert parsley! I'm sure you are rolling your eyes thinking "whoop di do! You found parsley. That's on every plate in upscale restaurants across America!" But alas my fair non-green hearted friends, this is not just any parsley, but an endangered one!

Again, you must be asking how is this my ace in the hole? This plant is considered endangered in the state of Washington. Therefore, federal law prohibits any kind of interactions that would adversely affect any endangered species. Which means you cannot build on that property! BAM! Eat that Russo. He has no idea.

They will keep me up to date, but after the lovely run in at the last one, I will not be going to any other court hearings. I really don't need to taunt Russo with my presence any more than I already have. He seems to have a large amount of patience, but I know that it is not infinite, and my mouth always seems to get the best of me. I would rather not test my theory that he would not attack me in public. I can be quite frustrating at times.

Just ask the guys in my kitchen. I am sitting outback in my favorite round chair. It is large, large enough to fit at least two people, and full of pillows. It hangs from the large tree in my fairy garden. It is my favorite place to sit outside and drink coffee. It's so quiet and peaceful.

Usually. It's not so peaceful right now. I can hear Jaxson and Paxton arguing in the kitchen. Over what? Only God knows. I have stopped paying them any attention. It's been a while since I left my house. Since I do not have much going on at work, and Karl heard of my lovely performance at the courthouse, I am pretty much being forced into hiding. I'm not allowed to go to work, I am not allowed to go to the gym, I am not allowed to go to the goddamn grocery store. The boys are taking turns rotating their shifts as well as food magically appearing in my kitchen.

Not that I care. I don't have much of an appetite anyway. I am feeling listless. I do not like being forced into a cage. That is why I am so far from home to begin with. I do not do well with someone telling me how I need to be living my life. It makes me want to give them the finger and prove otherwise. That is exactly what the boys are arguing over. I didn't listen to them the first time and put not just my life, but Jaxson's in danger too. It was enough of a rude awakening that I am not going to do something stupid like that again. I may be willing to put myself out there, but I couldn't live with myself if something happened to one of them because of me. Doesn't mean I have to like it though.

I hear a loud slam and cock my head towards the door. It's Paxton that is yelling.

"We need to do something! We can't just keep sitting here waiting for the boogeyman! Look at her man! Can you not see what this is doing to her? She is wasting away damn it! She is not eating, she barely sleeps, she just wanders around outside like nothing matters to her anymore. This is not who she is. Her fire is gone!"

I hear a glass shatter against a wall. Lovely. They are tearing up my kitchen. Sadly, I can't make myself seem to care. I do feel like I am wasting away. I feel bad that Paxton is so worried about me, but I am just biding my time. Trying to figure out how to end this. He is right, we can't just keep sitting on our asses. This needs to be over. I want my life back. I am going to hate it when this job ends because I am going to miss the boys. I must keep in mind though that this is exactly that. A job, to them.

Jaxson growl catches my attention. He hardly raises his voice; he doesn't need to. His presence is commanding enough on its own.

"Don't you fucking think I know that? Do you think I fucking enjoy seeing her like this? It's tearing me up inside, but until we get more information, we can't do a goddamn thing about it!"

I huff. It's nice to know they care, but I stop listening. I get up out of my chair and wander into my yard. It's so quiet and serene out here. I balked when I first came out here though. The seclusion I thought was a bit much. I thought that it was going to grate on me. I come from a loud boisterous family, so I am not so used to silence. I couldn't pass up on the house though. With the slight modifications I made after moving in, it is my dream house. I wasn't going to let it go. I searched long and hard to find some place that felt like home. House hunting is no joke. It is a long and miserable process that makes you feel like you need to settle for whatever you can find.

At that point in my life, I refused to settle though. So, I kept looking and held out till I found what I was looking for. It made me keep my apartment in the city longer than I wanted to, but it was totally worth it. Right about the time that I was about to give up and convince myself that I was just being too picky, my real estate agent sent me the listing. I knew instantly this was it.

It was an unusually quick sale. It was a vacation home for an older couple. They had recently died, and their children were not interested in keeping the property. They just wanted to get rid of it. It worked well in my favor. They took the first bid and signed the papers almost immediately. There was no need for the usual 30-day waiting period and all that jazz. The house was already empty and no one had been there in years.

As I am walking through the expanse of my front yard something strikes me as odd. I stop in my tracks and do a slow circle. It's quiet. Like really quiet. I don't hear any birds, or squirrels. Nothing is rustling in the trees. No crickets are chirping. That's odd. I am surrounded by forest. There is usually some kind of animal scurrying across the yard or trees. Something is up.

Chapter 20

Just as that thought occurs to me, I hear a clap of thunder. Crazy loud and super close. At the same time, I start to turn because I hear my front door slam open. I hear Jaxson roar my name and see him running towards me. Before I can ask him, what is going on, I feel something slam into me. As the white hot, searing pain rushes through me my first thought is that my favorite coffee cup just hit the ground and broke.

They say your life flashes before your eyes when you find yourself in a life-or-death situation. When you think, you are going to die. But that didn't happen to me. Everything did happen in what seemed like slow motion though. Watching my coffee cup fall, the coffee spilled out the sides as it tumbled through the air. The sound of Jaxson's feet pounding off my porch as he was running towards me. The burst of the birds out of the trees when the loud clap vibrated through the air. The thud my body made when it slammed back first into the ground.

I was in a daze while I was trying to figure out what the hell just happened, and why the hell I was in so much pain. While I was rolling my head around trying to shake the dark spots from my vision, I could hear more yelling. I couldn't make out what they were saying. All I could hear was ringing in my ears and my harsh pants from trying to catch my breath.

Jaxson came into view as his knees slid across the ground and up to my side.

"Percy! Oh fuck!"

He touches my shoulder and I scream. When he pulls his hand back quickly, I see it's covered in blood. Shit. I'm bleeding. It takes me entirely too long to put two and two together. It wasn't a clap of thunder that I heard, but a gunshot. I have been shot. Well, that would explain the searing pain and why I can not seem to move or feel my arm.

I vaguely see Paxton's feet go running across my yard towards the woods. Jaxson is screaming at him and screaming at someone on the phone. My vision is swimming and I think that I am going in and out of consciousness.

"Hang in there Kitten. Help is coming. Stay with me!"

He touches my face to try to get me to focus on him. I groan.

"You guys make getting shot look so fucking easy. This fucking sucks."

He chuckles a little.

"There you are, good. You keep talking to me. I'm sorry. This is going to hurt so fucking bad, but I need to touch you. I need to put pressure on your wound."

His eyes look so sad. Like it's hurting him as much as it's going to hurt me. He looked at me like that when he held me in the shower, and I was breaking down.

That was my last thought as he ripped his shirt off and pushed on the wound in my shoulder. I screamed again, but this time the pain was so bad that I blacked out.

I don't know how long I have been out, but I am still on the ground. It's cold. I can feel myself starting to shiver. Though I guess that can be from blood loss too. Jaxson is yelling at someone to fucking hurry and I feel him lean his head against my forehead.

"Please hold on. I can't lose you. I just found you. Please don't leave me. I haven't even told you how I feel yet. Stay with me. God I will do whatever you want me to do. I will give up everything. Just please don't take her from me."

He is whispering. Begging for my life. Tears slip out of the corners of my eyes. Not from the pain. From my heart breaking, listening to this man begging for me. He is so solid. So strong, and it's ripping me to shreds at how utterly lost he sounds. I don't want to die. I want to find out what he meant by that, but I don't think I have much of a say in the matter.

I want to wrap my arms around him and tell him everything is going to be fine, but I can't move. I am so cold. It's a strange feeling. The inability to make your body follow your commands. My mind is conscious, but my body feels detached. I guess I am in shock. Jaxson doesn't seem to notice that I am mildly coherent. He is still bent over me, shaking.

His head jerks up when he hears feet pounding towards him. When he looks up, he swings his arm around with his gun in hand. Some dude yells.

"Woah man. We're here to help. We need to get to her man. You need to back up."

He's holding both his hands up in the universal sign for surrender. Or in this case, chill the fuck out.

Lindsey is pulling Jaxson to the side and trying to calm him down. Telling him they are going to help me the best they can. Just let them do their job. Jax is yelling again and shoving Lindsey. I'm going in and out of consciousness again as the paramedics start strapping monitors to me and ripping my shirt off me. They are jerking me around and causing searing pain down my arm. It causes me to moan, and Jaxson jumps at them again with Lindsey holding him back.

"Be fucking careful you jackasses you are hurting her!"

"I'm sorry man. I am more worried about getting to her wounds as quickly as possible than her comfort. She's already turning blue. She's losing too much blood. We need to work quickly."

Jaxson roars as they are strapping me to the gurney, and they start running. I hear him whisper into the wind before everything goes black. "Please, just save her."

Chapter 21

I wake up to the super annoying sounds of monitors beeping. How they expect anyone to sleep through that shit I will never know. I know I am in the hospital. Laying on a rock-hard bed and looking like some kind of experiment with all the tubes coming out of me. What I don't know is how long I have been here.

I roll my head over, moving isn't going so well since I feel like I have been run over by a truck, and I see Jaxson slumped over in the chair next to my bed. He looks comical. He is way too big for that tiny chair. I am surprised he was able to shove himself into it at all and fall asleep. As I look him over, I notice that he looks really disheveled. His long hair is a mess, like he has been running his hands though it continuously, and his clothes are all wrinkled. If I am not mistaken, he is still wearing the same clothes he was in when I was shot. I guess I wasn't out for too long.

As I am staring at him the door to my room opens and my best friend walks in holding two cups of coffee. When she sees my eyes open, she screams and literally throws the coffee over her shoulder and runs over to my bed. I grunt when she slams into me. The jostling was not pleasant, and it hurt like a bitch, but she's clinging to me with tears running down her face so I can't hold it against her.

"You stupid Cunt waffle! I can't believe you almost died on me! What the actual fuck is going on?!? I come home to our street full of cops and the yard swarming with what looks like the damn swat team, and Jaxson completely losing his shit! What the fuck were you thinking getting shot!"

Before she can continue her tirade Jaxson pulls her off me. The screeching must have woken him. Gee I wonder why. The whole damn hallway is probably awake now with her chastising me for almost dying.

"Daphne. Enough! You are hurting her." Jaxson grunts at her. His voice thick with sleep. "Back off."

"Oh my god. Oh my god. I'm so sorry! I didn't even think. I didn't mean to hurt you. I was just so damn happy that you are awake and still with me. I have been going out of my mind with worry."

I grabbed her hand to stop her again.

"Daph. It's fine. I am ok. I feel like I have been run over by a truck. But I'm ok. You can relax."

The ruckus must have caught the ear of the nurses because while I am calming my, all but hysterical, best friend I hear a screech and a thud. We all look over to see one of the nurses lying on the floor in the middle of the puddle of coffee Daphne made by tossing them in the air over her shoulder.

"Oh shit!" Daphne rushes over to help the nurse get back on her feet. "Oh my god. I am so sorry! I didn't mean to make a mess. Here let me help you" She runs to the bathroom and grabs some towels and starts awkwardly wiping off the nurse's ass, trying to mop up her soaking wet scrubs.

"Uh. Sweetie. It's ok. Really. I'm fine."

Daphne is not listening, still in her tizzy. "Ma'am!" The nurse grabs her hand that is still patting her ass. "Really. You can stop that now. Though I do appreciate the action. It's been quite a while since anyone has paid so much attention to my hind quarters." Daphne's cheeks turn bright red, and I snort.

Which was a bad decision. If you've never snorted before, it's not dainty. It jostled my very aching body, hard. The pain makes me groan again. Stupid fucking Italian douche nozzles. I can't believe they shot me.

Well, I guess I can. They have been threatening me for quite a while now. But come on! How is this my life now? Never in a million years would I ever have believed that I was going to get shot. I am generally not this exciting.

The groan catches everyone's attention. Jaxson steps closer to me out of concern and Daphne looks like she is about to rush me again, but he grabs the back of her collar.

"No."

With the one word and the look on his face it makes her stop in her tracks. He does let the nurse get to me.

"Oh honey. I'm sorry. I got a little distracted there. I am Nurse Harmony. Let me check you out. How are you feeling?" She comes over to the side of the bed and starts pressing buttons on all the machines and squeezing IV bags.

"Not too shabby considering I got shot. Everything hurts though."

Jaxson growls at the reminder. He turns around and walks to the other side of the room with his fists clenching. He kind of looks like he wants to punch a wall right now. Which reminds me I need to ask him what he was talking about when he thought I was dying.

"Well, that's to be expected." Nurse Harmony starts fussing over me. She's fluffing my pillow and trying to make me more comfortable. "Let me go get some pain meds for you and I will let the Doctor know you are awake. He will want to talk to you. He's been waiting on you to wake up. We are all so glad to see those beautiful eyes of yours." She went out of the room as fast as she came in. This time stepping over the coffee puddle in the doorway.

Jaxson picks up the towels that Daphne was molesting the poor nurse with and starts cleaning up the mess. He is definitely the type to not do well with idle hands.

I look back over to Daphne who is still in the same spot that Jaxson made her freeze in, but she is twitching fiercely and biting on her lip.

"It's ok Daph. You can come over here. Just don't jump on me this time."

I wink at her, so she knows there was no harm done. I love her for her enthusiasm.

Chapter 22

The doctor came bustling in just a few minutes later. Taking long strides and moving a few degrees faster than normal people in everything he did. I guess that makes total sense though, being he is a saver of lives and all. You wouldn't be very good at your job if you just lollygagged around.

He's a good-looking man. He's tall and looks like he keeps himself in good shape, despite the fact that he most definitely doesn't have much down time. He is probably in his early forties. I'm guessing his age by the small smattering of grey hair at his temples. His face is smooth and has no wrinkles, but he does have some laugh lines in the corners of his eyes. Which to me is a great sign of his character, and amazing genes. It means he has laughed a lot in his lifetime. With that tidbit and his looks, I can safely bet that his bedside manner is much appreciated by all the female population.

He walks up to the side of my bed with his hand outstretched.

"Ah. Mrs. Persephone. Absolutely love the name, by the way. I would wager to guess that it is very fitting. My name is Dr. Brigid. You can call me Brendan."

Jax growls a little at the fact the doctor is holding my hand a little longer than is normally socially acceptable for strangers. I didn't really notice at first though. My head is cocked to the side while I am thinking hard. His name struck a very fuzzy memory I am trying to think of.

I snort then. It came to me. He has a twinkle in his eye when he realizes what conclusion I came to. "Your name is very fitting as well.

Slight accent, and your name is Brendan Brigid. I would wager you are Irish, but you have been over here for quite some time."

"You would be correct Miss." He has let go of my hand at this point and is shining his very annoying light pen in my eyeballs and checking my bandages. "How are you feeling? I assume, considering your trauma, not that great, but are you in a lot of pain? Do you need some stronger pain meds? Do you remember what happened?"

It takes a second longer than I would like to process the rapid-fire questions. With a slow blink I take a second to let my mind catch up.

"You would be correct. Yes. Absolutely, and unfortunately." I answer with a small nod. Go me! I think I answered all of those.

Dr. Brigid chuckles with my nod. "Short and sweet. I like it. I can help with the pain. We want to stay ahead of that. Being in too much pain will hinder your healing process. All your stats look good. I am confident that you are one lucky lady and will heal with little to no aftereffects of your injuries. You were incredibly lucky in terms of getting shot. They hit no major arteries, and it was a through and through. So that's fantastic."

Before he can continue, Jaxson is growling like a freaking bear at him.

"Lucky? There's nothing fucking lucky about getting shot! It should never have happened. I was supposed to protect her, and she got fucking shot right in front of my goddam eyes!" His chest is heaving, and he is approaching Dr. Brigid like he was the one that shot me.

To his credit, he doesn't flinch at all from Jaxson's aggression. I don't give him a chance to respond though. Jaxson has finally gotten close enough for me to reach him. All it takes is me putting my hand lightly on his arm and he freezes instantly.

I whisper. "Hey. It's not his fault, and it's not yours either. I have been heavily monitored by all of you. There was no way to know that that was going to happen. I don't blame any of you. We knew they were going to make a move eventually. At least it's out in the open now."

Jaxson huffs but doesn't pull away. He takes a step closer to me and runs his knuckles lightly down the side of my face. "It shouldn't have happened. It's killing me that it did happen. It should be me in that bed, not you. Never you." He shakes his head roughly and walks away. He walks out the door without a second glance.

Dr. Brigid clears his throat. "Well. That one is a bit intense now isn't he."

Daphne snorts. "Doc. You have no idea."

Chapter 23

The last week has been a whirlwind of activity. I have spent every waking moment doing what I can to get out of the hospital. I have been constantly surrounded by people, beeping machines, oh god the beeping, and being poked and prodded and tortured by the devil himself. I.e the physical therapist.

"Uuuuuuugh! For the love of God. I swear you really are Satan himself. Why do you love torturing me so!"

I half screech at David, my Physical Therapist.

"Oh. Hush. Stop your whining. I know that you are completely fine. You will get no sympathy from me. You stormed in here telling me to do whatever it is that I had to do to get you out of here. That is exactly what I have been doing. You don't get out of here without me saying so, so if I were you I would do a lot less name calling and a lot more diligently following directions." He winks at me as he turns around.

"I mean, I heart your face and you are the sweetest thing and I think you helping me is so amazing and I so do NOT know what I would do without you!"

David bends over at the waist and smacks his thigh. He is laughing so hard. 'I'm kidding, sweet cheeks. I have already signed all the necessary paperwork to release you today. As long as you keep doing the stretches that we have worked on this week, you will be just fine. I think you can do them by yourself at home now."

He is handing me a packet of papers as Pax saunters into the room. "Absolutely Doc! I will make sure she keeps doing everything she is supposed to be doing." He smirks at David and slings his arm around my shoulder.

I try really hard not to grimace. I don't want David to think that I am in too much pain to leave, but holy cow does my stupid shoulder still hurt and this big ogre is slinging me around like its nothing.

So I smack him. Hard. Right in the stomach. He curls over with the impact.

"Ouch! What was that for?"

"Shoulder Duffus. I'm still a little achy."

The second I say the word shoulder he is jumping away from me like I am going to catch him on fire. "Oh shit. Sorry! I can't believe I Just did that."

His face is red with embarrassment as I start walking by him. "It's fine Pax. Let's just go. I really want to get the hell out of here. Go home and take a real shower and sleep in my own bed for once, and I am sure Panda has been going nuts without me being home."

"Well, I can do that Darlin'. I already have the car pulled up to the front door and all your things inside already. Panda has been just fine thank you very much. We have been getting along famously. Thanks, David, for springing her." He shakes his hand as I wave, speed walking to the door.

David just chuckles. He has grown quite used to my quirkiness by now.

"No problem, man. I hate to see her go. She has been, by far, my funnest client, but I am glad to help."

Paxton starts jogging to catch me. I really am burning rubber to get the hell out of this hospital. I don't want to have to spend another second in this place and I now have the papers to get me out of here. I am wasting no time. He will just have to keep up.

Either Paxton or Daphne have been with me everyday that I have been stuck here. They have been sweet doing everything they can to keep me comfortable and not lonely in this hell hole.

Have I mentioned how much I hate the hospital? No? Well, I do. Vehemently.

I can't appreciate them enough by doing everything they have for me, but man am I ready for some solitude. I just want to be able to take a damn shower by myself.

Jaxson hasn't shown his face again since he walked out on me after my surgery. I'm not sure why, but if I had to guess I would bet it's from self deprecation. He can't stand to fail, and he feels like he has by me getting shot.

I, of course, think that is absolutely ludicrous. There is no way that any of them could have predicted what happened. If they had any more security measures on me, I would have been chained to my toilet. I am pretty sure I have more freaking security measures on me then the damn president. Ok, maybe not that much, but they have been thorough.

I am kind of surprised that someone managed to slip through anything at my own home, but I don't blame anyone. It had been such a long time since we had heard anything from Russo or his men that I had forgotten what the boys were doing hanging out with me. We had all relaxed. Well maybe not Jax. I don't think the man knows what that word means.

I guess we won't forget now. Aside from the fact that my shoulder will be a constant reminder, I am pretty sure that I may very well be chained to a toilet when I get back home while they figure out how to catch these guys.

I mentally roll my eyes. My life really has become a freaking scene out of The God Father.

I see the light of all the glass doors that mark the entrance to the hospital. Or in my case, the exit. I started walking faster and dragging Paxton by the arm.

"Come on Pax. Take me home."

Chapter 24

I t's a little surreal being back home. We're pulling into the driveway, and I haven't been able to look away from my yard. Paxton is chatting away amicably, probably trying to distract me, but I am not hearing a word of it.

All I am hearing is the thunderclap of the gunshot that threw me across the ground. Paxton parks the car and instead of heading to my front door, I started walking over to the spot it all happened.

"Hey where are you going Darlin'?" Pax is shouting at me nervously.

I don't even look over my shoulder to tell him to give me a minute. I am kind of in a trance meandering through my yard with my thoughts running wild. I can't really decide if I am traumatized or simply curious.

As I get to the spot that is a little darker from my blood, I stare at the ground silently. It's weird to realize that it is my blood, but I don't really feel traumatized.

I've never seen myself as a victim, and Russo has already taken a swing at me once. That first encounter kind of knocked the shock out of me. Now I am fully aware of what kind of man he is and what to expect from him.

Huh, well that's cool. I was a little worried that I was going to feel uncomfortable in my own home. I am relieved that I can honestly say that I am ok. I am angry as hell. But I am not broken this time.

With that thought, I turn around and walk back toward my house. Paxton is pacing back and forth on my porch. Mumbling to himself. He couldn't decide whether he should chase me down or let me have a moment. He looked surprised when he realized that I already had my moment before he got to decide.

I patted his shoulder as I walked past him. "I am fine Pax. I really am. Stop worrying so much. I promise I am not going to be a sniveling mess.'

"Darlin' it's ok to not be ok. You had a very traumatizing experience. No one expects you to bounce back immediately. It'll take some time."

"That's just it Paxton. I really don't need time. I am not traumatized. I got that out of the way when they tried to run me off the road. I am not surprised either. I am just irritated now. I want this asshole caught and out of my face, so I don't have to deal with this shit anymore, but I am not traumatized. I swear. I am fine."

"Uh huh. All men know that when a woman says she is fine, she is really not fine. Fine never means fine. Fine means that something is very much not fine, they just don't want to say it. But you can say it. I can take it."

"Paxton." I wave my hand in front of his face. "You need to take it down a notch. You are starting to sound like me." That made him stop.

"Damn. That's never good. Go take a shower. I am going to throw your shit in the washer because it all smells sterile like the hospital and I'll get some dinner started."

"Sounds like a plan to me."

As I turn around to start walking towards my bedroom, I hear the loud screeching war cry of Panda flying at my face.

"Oh shit!" I go to brace myself with the impact knowing damn well this is going to hurt like a son of a bitch. But when she gets going there is no stopping her. She is an overweight tiny little freight train.

It takes a second for me to open my eyes that I had scrunched shut and realize that there was never any pain. She's still screeching trying to get to me, but Jaxson had walked into the room right at that moment and had caught her straight out of the air before she had slammed into my chest.

"Now girl. You need to calm down. Your mama is injured, and you can't go throwing yourself at her like that because it is really going to hurt her. I know you missed her, but I can't let you go until I know that you are going to be gentle."

Jaxson was gently stroking Panda's head, getting her to chill the hell out. I am second guessing myself believing that I am not traumatized and think that I may be hallucinating. Jaxson was never this affectionate with Panda before, and you could most definitely tell that he is from Texas just then. He sounded as bad as Pax does. Not to mention I haven't seen him in a week, so I am kind of taken aback by him being here to begin with.

In the middle of my internal rambling, he had managed to get her to calm down and he was gently handing her over to me. She immediately holds onto my face with both her paws and begins rubbing the side of her face against mine.

"It's ok girl. I am fine. I missed you too. But damn you are heavy. I can tell no one forgot to feed you while I was gone." At that she lightly smacked me and jumped down and ran. I swear I heard her huff on her way back into her tree house. I shake my head. "She is way too domesticated."

I start walking again back toward my room and my shower. I don't even look over my shoulder when I start speaking to Jaxson. "I am surprised you're even here. Considering I haven't seen hide nor hair of you in a week."

He gently grabs my good arm and makes me stop to look at him. He had a pleading look in his eyes when he looked down at me.

"Hey. I know. I am sorry. I have no excuse for not coming back to check on you. It was completely selfish of me. I was having a hard time accepting what happened and didn't want to take my frustration out on you. I spent the week chained to my desk combing over every word of intel we have on Russo and his men. Trying to find something that I may have missed to give me a clue to his hideout. I called Paxton everyday to check on you and see how you were doing."

I pulled my arm out of his grip. "It's fine Jaxson. You don't have to babysit me. I will tell you what I told Pax. I really am ok. I have faith you will figure it out. You are hard enough on yourself; you won't hear it from me too. I just want to take a shower. You do whatever it is that you need to do to make yourself feel better about this situation."

He huffed a bitter laugh. "Feel better? You think that there is anything that is going to make me feel better that you got fucking shot while I was supposed to be protecting you?"

He takes a step closer to me and growls. "There is not a goddamn thing on this planet that is ever going to make me feel better about this. Ever. The only thing I can do is catch this bastard. And make sure that it damn well never happens again."

I just nod. I don't know what to say to him. There's nothing I can say anyway. He's a dog with a bone and there's nothing anybody can do to take it from him till he finds whatever it is that he is looking for.

His eyes soften. "Go. Shower. I'll make sure that you have food and coffee when you get out."

I moan at the mention of coffee. "Sweet holy nectar of the gods, I have missed me some good coffee!"

I skip towards the shower, a lot less worried about soaking in the water and more excited to get it over with so I can have a decent cup of joe. The sludge they tried to give me at the hospital was not even worthy to be called coffee, much less drinkable. I hear Jaxson chuckle under his breath as I close the bathroom and I swear I hear him whisper "Damn I have missed you, Kitten." I must be hearing things though. Jaxson has never been that sentimental with me.

Chapter 25

The idea of taking a shower sounded fantastic but the logistics of it when you are one armed makes it a lot more difficult than I originally thought. I was huffing and puffing and highly irritated before I even got into the shower. It took me ten damn minutes to even get my clothes off. Trying to work my shirt and my bra off one handed kept twinging my shoulder and it freaking hurt! You really don't appreciate the help of good nurses until you don't have them with you anymore.

Once I had finally actually made it into the shower, I thought that I was home free, but noooooo. I realized I now must tackle the mess that is my hair. I have a lot of it. How the hell am I going to get this shit properly cleaned one handed. The nurse helped wash it while I was in the hospital, but I wasn't able to actually condition it well so it was a mess. I wasn't going to complain, like I said, I just wanted out of there. I didn't really care about my hair at the time, but damn if I don't get a handle on this soon some birds are going to be trying to make homes on the top of my head.

I must have smacked my head against the side of the shower out of exasperation and cussed louder than I meant to because Jaxson came busting in the bathroom door.

"Kitten! Are you ok? Did you fall?"

I sighed heavily. "Yes Jax. I'm fine. No, I didn't fall. It's all good."

"Then what's wrong? You were cursing and I heard a loud noise like you fell."

"Why is it that you always see me in the shower in some of my most vulnerable moments? You must find me so weak? It's nothing really. It's quite stupid if you think about it. With everything going on. I just got shot, but I am irritated about my hair."

He's silent for so long I look over my shoulder at him. He has his back to me. Ever the gentleman. Trying to give me some semblance of privacy even though he busted up in the bathroom with me naked in the shower. Again.

"Your hair?" He finally gets out, quite obviously very confused.

"I'm one armed. Took me struggling 10 minutes to even get my clothes off to get into the damn shower. I just need to fucking wash and condition my damn hair. I have a lot of hair. I can't comb it if I don't condition it. Not that I could fucking comb it right now any way. I can only use one damn arm. But the damn birds are going to make nests in my damn hair soon. It's gross. I feel gross. And I was so damn looking forward to just having a good god damn shower and finally being clean and not smelling like a damn hospital, but I can't because of my stupid fucking arm."

I thump my head against the side of the shower again. I jump a little when I feel his hand touch my back.

"Shhh Kitten. I don't think you're weak, the opposite. I think you're one of the strongest people I know. Let me help. I've got you."

He turns my back to him as he begins to work the shampoo through my hair. Meticulously massaging it through the mass of hair into my scalp. It feels divine. It makes me a little weak in the knees.

We stand in silence as he completely focuses on his job. He washes my hair, rinses it out and then works the conditioner in. He must have noticed my comb that was hanging in my shower as well because he even took the time to work all the tangle out of my hair while the conditioner was working its magic. I wouldn't have even known what to have said even if he did want to talk. I would have expected this kind of attention from Paxton, but not Jaxson.

But as soon as that thought passed through my mind, I realized that no that's not right. Not, when it comes to me. Jaxson has shown nothing but kindness to me since I have met him. He seemed a bit standoffish and hard to get to know. Well, in actuality, I don't really know all that much about him, but in my most vulnerable moments it has been him that has picked me up. That has taken care of me.

He has been attentive to me in his gruff sort of way, but I still don't know if that is because he is really good at his job, or if it's because it's me personally. He could just be extremely dedicated to his work. I mean, he didn't come to see me at all while I was at the hospital. He said he was still working, and I don't doubt he was. He said he "checked in with Pax everyday about me" but that doesn't exactly scream adoration. Ugh, he's so infuriating. Damn sexy, but infuriating.

I need to not get attached. I'm just a job to him. Once he catches Russo he will be gone. On to the next job. Taking care of the next girl he must protect. No, that doesn't make my insides scream with jealousy or anything. Don't get attached. This man has the potential to crack my heart wide open.

With that thought I stepped away from him and clear my throat. I go to rinse my hair out, keeping my back to him.

"Um. Can you hand me a towel? Thanks for helping."

"You're welcome. Don't struggle so hard next time. Just ask for help."

I can feel the confusion coming off him with my sudden shift of mood. We just had a moment, but emotions are running high right now and I can't be sure that this thing, whatever it is, is not just out of guilt for me getting shot.

In this moment, I need to protect myself from Jaxson as much as I do from Russo. Each man has the potential to filet me alive for two very different reasons. I'm not sure which one would be worse either.

Chapter 26

After I have managed to wrestle myself back into some clothes, I make my way back out into the kitchen following the delicious smells of real food and coffee. I involuntarily moan when I realize I am about to have some real coffee after what seems like forever, when in actuality it was only a handful days in the hospital.

Paxton hands me a cup the way I like it before I even have to ask. "Oh, sweet baby Jesus I have missed youuuuuuuu."

"Darlin' I believe that is all kind of sacrilegious." He says laughing at me as he watches me caress my cup of coffee.

I glared at him. "You should know by now no one comes between me and my coffee Pax."

He just keeps laughing.

I see out of the corner of my eye Jaxson is leaning up against the wall just watching the exchange as usual. Keeping his distance. It doesn't make it any easier trying to decipher his feelings.

"Sit Darlin' You need to eat too before I can give you your meds and the boss man is on his way to decide what our next step is gonna' be."

I opened my mouth to start asking questions, but he just shoves my fork in my mouth.

"Just wait. Eat. You'll be able to ask any questions after we get all the information, alright."

I glare at him while I chew the too big bite he purposely shoved in my mouth and he just laughed me and went over to the kitchen to start setting up their makeshift command station.

I CONTINUE TO SLOWLY eat my dinner while I watch Lindsey, Paxton, and Jaxson go back and forth and argue scenarios with each other. Shoot each other down and continue the cycle over again.

They have all their big boy toys, what I call all their computers and security tech gear, out going over all their current intel on all the movements on Russo's guys that they have been able to pull since my shooting and essentially come up with diddly squat and no one was happy about it.

It was making them all agitated. Russo was giving them a run for their money, and they weren't used to it. Apparently, they were used to being the top dogs and not having to work this hard to catch their mark and starting to take their frustrations out on each other.

It was starting to annoy me. I was getting tired of listening to them bickering. They were just going in circles and not being productive. Clearly, they have run out of ideas.

"Use me as bait."

They were arguing with each other so loudly they didn't hear me. So, I cleared my throat and tried again louder.

"Use me as bait."

That worked. Silence. All three heads swiveled towards me in unison. Matching looks of incredulousness on their faces.

"Absolutely fucking not!" Paxton yelled.

"No chance in hell." Lindsey said calmly.

"Out of the question." Jaxson took a step towards me like he was going to shake some sense into me.

"Well at least you guys are finally agreeing on something and not wasting time yelling at each other. But what other choice do you have? You don't. You have exhausted all other options. You literally can't find him. He is in the wind like you said. I trust you guys to protect me. Use your assets. He wants me. Let him think he can have me." I shrugged.

Jaxson got in my face, "You trust us to protect you? You've been in a high-speed car chase, run off the road, dragged out of a car, almost abducted and god knows what else, and ACTUALLY shot! How can you even say that? We haven't protected you at all!"

Paxton grabbed him and pulled him away from me. "Alright brother. Point made. None of us are thrilled by this idea, but you don't need to be scaring her any worse alright."

"I'm fine Pax. He doesn't scare me. I know he won't hurt me. I'm still here Jaxson. Russo doesn't have me. You HAVE protected me. And again, you don't have any other choice. I want this over with. I'm tired of sitting around waiting for him on the defense. It's time to MAKE something happen. I still think all this shit is insane. I'm a damn environmentalist for Pete's sake" I huff.

I glare at Paxton. "You know this makes sense. It should be my choice anyway."

I walk off and go outside and leave them to go back to their arguing. I just want things to go back to normal. I just want my life back. I am over all the insanity and constantly being monitored. I want to go back to being a nobody and my life being boring and safe.

I can't lie to myself though and say that I am not going to miss having the guys in my life though. I was mostly alone before. Daphne is gone all the time because of her job. I am going to miss the company sometimes. As much as Paxton gets on my nerves sometimes, he's like having a little brother. I am going to miss him calling me Darlin' him joking around and constantly putting a smile on my face.

Lindsey isn't around as much, but when he is, his presence is reassuring. Like a big brother. It's hilarious watching him with Paxton and how Pax rubs on his nerves on purpose to try to get him to loosen up a bit. To try to get him out of his boss man roll and to have a little fun. He takes his job very seriously, but these guys are brothers to each other, and you see it in how they interact with each other.

Strong broody Jaxson. Somehow has wormed his way closer and closer into my heart and I am putting a stop to that now. As much as I want to keep him, I know I can't. If they wise up and take my suggestion, we will finally nail Russo and be done with this shit. Then he will be done with me.

Chapter 27

As I'm staring out into my yard trying to imagine what life is going to be like without the guys in it when it goes back to "normal" I had tuned out the guys in the house arguing with each other again so I didn't notice when I was no longer alone.

I startled hard when someone lays a hand on my shoulder. "Shit!" and whip around expecting it to be Paxton coming out to check on me or something. I was even more shocked when it was Jaxson.

"Sorry Kitten. Didn't mean to scare you."

I had my hand over my chest trying to will my heart to slow back down. I guess it was not a very smart move to be so unaware of my surroundings when I have a crazy psychopath currently out trying to murder me, but I guess having a house full of security dudes gives you a false sense of security.

"It's fine. I was off in my own little world. Not your fault. What's Up?"

"I wanted to apologize. For yelling at you. I let my emotions get the better of me. I just can't stand the thought of seeing you get hurt again. It would kill me, Kitten. It almost killed me the last time."

I kind of just stood there blinking at him. This was not what I expected.

Jax is looking at me with a rather intense look on his face. He's always pretty intense though so I don't think much of it. It's different this time, at the moment, the look he has in his eyes is saying something to me that I don't understand. There are some underlying emotions there that aren't normally, but I've learned not to push him. He will only speak when he is ready to. So, I just take a breath and wait him out.

There is no telling what is going to come out of his mouth. Usually, it's some sort of chiding me for doing something rash (he's probably going to lecture me about the bait situation), or not taking something seriously enough. A grunt here and there. I say that jokingly because he has been quite a bit more vocal lately than he used to be. Helping someone deal with multiple attempts on their life will do that to a person, I guess.

I have come to rely so much on him, I don't know what I am going to do when he is gone. I don't really remember what life was like without him. It seems like he has always been a part of my life now. His silence and strength is comforting in a way that I know no matter what, he will always be there for me. All of this even though I am fairly certain I annoy the crap out of him most of the time. We really are complete opposites, but maybe that is why I feel like he completes me in a way that nobody else has. Which makes it all that much harder to try not to get attached to him.

As all this is flying through my brain like a spider monkey, I raise my eyebrow and open my mouth to ask him why he is looking at me all crazy, but he beats me to it. What comes out of his mouth shocks the holy bejeezus out of me.

He says "I want to love you till you're no longer lonely..."

There's a couple of beats of silence because I am totally taken aback. That most definitely was not what I was expecting to come out of his mouth.

"You... You want to... Wait, were those song lyrics? Did you just quote song lyrics to me? I mean that's super adorable, but totally not what I would expect from you. I'm pretty sure that's a song though..."

He grabs my face and tilts it up to look at him and he cuts me off mid ramble.

"Puppies are adorable. Men are not adorable. You know what, I don't even know why I tried."

He drops his hands from my face and for the second time in less than ten minutes I'm completely taken aback. I am not even sure what is going on at this point in time.

"Wha... WHat? Why would you say that? I know I'm kind of weird and maybe sometimes hard to love. I have a lot of quirks and ramble sometimes. And I know I haven't dated in a while, but surely, I'm not completely unlovable."

My heart has sunk. This man is putting me through the wringer right now. I have been trying to convince myself for a while to not get attached (while totally getting attached) to this sexy giant, then he comes out here, throws this line out like I think he is trying to tell me loves me then says oh wait never mind. Like what the hell?

He tilts my face back towards him because I am now depressingly staring at my feet.

"Kitten. Look at me. You are a strong, smart, beautiful woman. You have the biggest heart out of anyone that I have ever met. You absolutely deserve to be loved. Completely and fully. To a point that you would never have to ask that question again. I wasn't talking about you. I meant me. I'm not romantic. I don't know why I tried to be."

My heart starts to beat a little quicker.

"Oh. OOOOh. Damn it! I ruined your moment, didn't I? Wait! Start over. Please, what was that you were saying? You're totally romantic!"

He chuckles at me and silently shakes his head. I'm trying to be quiet, but maybe squirming a little with the effort. Was he going to tell me he is in love with me? That would be completely amazing because I have had the hots for him from the second that I saw him, but he's always been so quiet and serious. Surely, he can't be in love with my kind of crazy. I really thought that he was just dedicated to his job, and it had nothing to do with me personally, but maybe he is into me.

While I am in the middle of my silent rambling, again, in my head he cuts me off again. He doesn't say anything though. He just grabs my face and pulls me to him and kisses me. The most mind-blowing, toe-curling kiss, Holy Jesus! This man can kiss! I guess what they say about the quiet ones is true.

After what seems like an eternity, yet not long enough, he releases me. I'm still somewhat in a daze. He literally kissed me stupid right now. Jax says very seriously,

"Yes. Yes, you deserve to be loved. I don't know why. You drive me crazy most of the time, but for whatever reason I am in love with you. If it takes me telling you everyday how amazing you are to get you to believe it, I will do it without a second thought."

He cracks a half smile.

"Hell of a time for you to be growing a sense of humor Mister, but I'll take it!"

I reached up to pull him down to kiss me again. I can barely wrap my arms around him because he is so big compared to me. He puts his hands under my ass and lifts me up so I can wrap my legs around his waist. Holy Hades that is hot! He holds me up like it is nothing.

In the middle of me being totally blissed out and not caring if the world around me burns, I hear.

"Oh shit! Yeeeeeeeah! Good job Jax!"

Jaxson slowly sets me back on my feet and I roll my eyes and turn around.

"Really Paxton. You had to go and ruin my moment!"

"Sorry not sorry. I was wondering when you were going to get the balls to admit that you were in love with her. I thought that I was going to have to kiss her in front of you to get you to own up to it." Paxton laughs.

"DON'T YOU FUCKING THINK about it." Jaxson almost growls at him.

"See! Getting punched in the face would have been totally worth it!" Paxton starts to laugh as he's jumping out of Jaxson's reach.

I sigh heavily. Well, there goes my moment.

Chapter 28

We all made our way back inside after Pax so rudely popped my happy bubble. I'm still floating on cloud nine in disbelief that I may not be losing Jaxson after we catch this son of bitch after all. I still can't believe that he just told me he loves me. Because of Paxton's interruption, I didn't get a chance to say anything back.

I freeze while the boys are discussing what they do. I never said anything back. Did I offend him? Is he going to take everything back because he feels like I don't feel the same? Shit, the one time my motor mouth fails me, and I may have blown it.

Jaxson must have sensed my panic because I snapped out of my inner terror to feel him lifting my chin to look at him. "Kitten, what is it? What's wrong?"

"Nothing. Nothing."

With a quick shake of my head, I'm attempting to dispel the panic and get my head back in the game. It is way more important right now to convince these big lugs to use me as bait against Russo than my love life is. I am just going to cling to the hope that I can get a moment alone with Jaxson again soon so we can talk about things.

He raises an eyebrow at my continued silence. "Are you sure? You don't look fine." I look him square in the face so he can see that I am serious.

"Yes. I am fine. Let's focus on what I need to do to convince you guys that using me as bait is the best viable option that we have."

That causes silence to fall over the room and the tension to be palatable. I see all three of their mouths start to open in protest, so I stick my hand up to try and stop the tirade before it starts.

I take a deep breath and sigh.

"Look. Am I bursting with joy at the idea of putting myself directly in the path of a psycho? No. It has not been any fun for me to get my car totaled, killed a man, and then subsequently getting shot in front of my own home. But I am not naive. These things are just going to keep happening until Russo either gets what he wants or gets me out of the way."

I run my hands through my hair and start pacing back and forth. So far, they are remaining silent and letting me have my piece. Which I do not trust at all. No matter what I have to say, I know that Jaxson at the very least is going to buck hard against willingly putting me in danger. I can't blame him. I am internally freaking out, but I know it is the best option that we have. As good as these guys are, they are the best at what they do, and they still can not find out where or what these guys are or what they are going to do next.

I stop pacing and put my hands on my hips. "I am not going to pretend that I know anything more than you guys about catching the bad guys, but this is my life. I know that this is not going to be easy, I know that it is going to be scary, I know that there is a lot of potential for disaster, but you can't tell me that there is a better option."

It's so quiet in the room that you can hear the crickets outside. Even Panda feels the tension. She was about to come looking for snacks but took one foot into the kitchen and slowly started backing up. She ran across the room and leaped headfirst into her tree. All you could see of her now was the light glaring off her eyeballs. I feel you Panda, I feel you.

I turn away from Panda and back towards Jaxson.

"Please. You have to see reason. Just let me do this."

It comes out as a whisper. He turns away from and looks at Pax and Lindsey. Right about the time that I think I am going to have to change tactics and throw a hissy fit to get my way, he opens his mouth.

"If this is even going to be an option, and that's a big if. We need to come up with the best plan to get her in and out. Then plan B, and C, and D. I will not. Will not. Put Percy in danger if I am not one hundred percent positive that we can get this done without her getting a scratch on her."

Cue mental high five to myself. Yes! We are about to get shit done. I am one step closer to getting my goddamn life back.

Chapter 29

My early excitement has quickly waned. I am currently leaning over the bar in my kitchen, laying on my arm, and nursing, I don't even know what number, cup of coffee.

These guys have been going in circles for hours. Paxton or Lindsey will come up with some sort of viable plan and Jaxson will quickly and efficiently blast holes in it with everything that could go wrong and wipe it off the table as a possible option.

I know Pax and Lindsey are way past getting frustrated and are totally about to lose their shit. I have been rather impressed by the amount of patience that they have had, but I think everyone is at the end of their rope right now. I need to step in and make these guys take a break before someone snaps and they come to blows.

I really like my furniture, and I have no doubt that it would be completely destroyed if all this tension erupts and these guys start taking their frustrations out on each other. My house may be open, but these men I swear are direct descendants of some vikings and already take up enough space just sitting here.

I clap my hands loudly to get their attention.

"Hey! Giant pieces of man meat standing in my dining room!"

That seems to catch their attention because they finally stop arguing and look in my direction. As the smile slowly starts growing on Paxton's face, I know he's about to have some idiotic retort that is just going to piss Jax off all over again. So, I lift my hand up to stop him before he can even begin.

"Look, you have been going at it for hours. You are just getting frustrated and ALL of you have your hackles up and are not accomplishing anything. You need to take a break. Take a breather and we can refocus and start again later. It is not doing anyone any good just arguing and pissing each other off. I know there is no easy solution, and this is going to take some creative thinking, but you're not going to figure it out tonight. How about we reconvene in the morning after you guys clear your heads and we can start over with some rational thinking. Maybe get Eddy in here also so he can throw his two cents in. I bet he would be able to help a ton with his side of expertise."

"Well hot damn darlin'. I think that is the most logical thing I have ever heard you say. It's a scary day when you're being more levelheaded than we are."

I am counting the seconds in my head because I know Jaxson is about to smack Pax in the back of the head. Three, two, one. There it is. I shake my head as Paxton chuckles and starts to pack up all the computers strewn all over my kitchen table.

Before they leave they, all agree on a time to meet tomorrow to get together and start discussing what it means to use me as bait and if they can come up with a safe option. Jax has made it abundantly clear that this is not even going to be an option if he does not get convinced that they can even do this without me coming to anymore harm. I generally would be terrified at the idea of possibly being taken or injured, but after already being run off the road, almost getting kidnapped, and then shop in my own home, I am more than over this whole situation and am willing to do whatever it takes to just be done with this mob bullshit.

I tell them all bye and watch them pack up and leave and try to get myself situated to just go to bed and end this chaotic day. My mind is running a million miles an hour and I have no idea how I am going to manage to shut down and actually sleep. It seems like for the millionth time, I think to myself how is this my life now?

Chapter 30

I am predictably lying in bed, wide awake, staring at my ceiling. After having the boys over and all the arguing going on, my house just seems too quiet. I can hear Panda snoring away in her treehouse like a little freight train and usually that comforts me, but tonight I can't seem to relax.

While I am replaying all the arguments for strategies as using me for bait, I hear the quiet click of my front door latching shut. Is Daphne home? I could have sworn she let me know that she was going to be hunkering down in her office tonight for some last-minute preparations for some event she was about to have. Plus, she is never that quiet.

I sit up in my bed to strain to hear anything else. My entire body begins to shake when I hear light footsteps coming towards my bedroom door. Did we hesitate too long on making plans to be on the offensive side of this and Russo sent another henchmen after me. Is he bold enough to just blindly slip into my house? Without a second thought I answered that question with a resounding yes. They shot me in my own front yard with my security team with me. Of course, he would come after me when I was all alone and not expecting it. He probably has men watching me at all times, reporting my every move.

Before my dumbass even gets to the part of my mental ramblings where I ACTUALLY come up with an escape plan to save myself, my bedroom door starts to slowly open. Fuck, fuck, fuck, what am I going to do? Take him. That's what I am going to do. It's only one dude. He's probably big, and probably has killed a lot of people, but I took self-defense so I wouldn't be helpless. In this situation. If nothing else, I am going to put up a goddamn fight and not go easily. He's going to have to work at taking me that's for sure. I am little, but my frustration and anger over this stupid situation is warrior sized. Bring it on mother fucker!

I slowly lay back to look like I am sleeping so I can take this fucker by surprise. I'm listening hard to see if I can pinpoint where he is in my room. The sound of heavy boots softly hitting the floor perks my ears off. Did he just take his shoes off? What the hell? Next the distinct sound of a zipper. Oh, hell no! Run me off the road, shoot me, fine, but you are not going to try to rape me.

Now is the time to use surprise to my advantage so I take it. I quickly jump and yell "Not today mother fucker! Your pencil dick will be going nowhere near my lady garden!" I slam into a hard chest and start pounding anywhere I can touch. As I reach the level of squirrel on cocaine, I hear my name being yelled between grunts.

"Percy!" Grunt. "Kitten!" Grunt. "It's me Jax. Calm down!"

It finally registers I am currently pummeling the shit out of Jaxson. My hand is still raised, and I hit him again for good measure. "You fucker! What the hell is wrong with you?!!? I thought someone was trying to murder me in my sleep!"

I stopped hitting him, but I am mildly hyperventilating now as my whole body is shaking now. Coming off an adrenaline high is no joke. I'm trying to take deep breaths and calm my racing heart when he approaches me, hands raised. Slowly.

"I am so goddam sorry kitten. I am an idiot. I wasn't even thinking about how this would look. I just needed to get to you. I came in so quietly that in case you were asleep I didn't want to wake you. I was just planning on crawling into bed and holding you, so I knew you were safe. All this strategizing about using you as bait has set me so far on edge I think if I grind my teeth any harder, they're going to end up dust in my mouth."

"As sweet as that is, maybe don't sneak into my house when there is a crazed mob boss out there trying to take me out. You almost game me a damn heart attack."

He's rubbing up and down my arms and pulls me into his chest. "I know kitten. I wasn't thinking. But I am damn proud with how fast you reacted and took me by surprise." He uses his finger to lift my chin, like he always does, so he's looking me in the eyes. "Good girl. Don't take anything laying down. Fight like hell. I just found you, I don't know what I would do if I lost you."

That makes me melt into a pile of goo. It also makes me smile extra hard because it reassures me that I really did hear things right when I was bleeding out on the ground, and he was begging for my life. I stand on my tip toes to kiss him.

"I was going to do everything in my power to take you down. Like a rabid animal." He chuckles. "But next time, text me babe. I feel like I just lost 5 years off my life from sheer terror."

He just grunts as he's guiding me back towards the bed. I get back under the blanket and he curls around me from behind. Wrapping his arm around my hips and pulling me as close to him and he can possibly get.

"I just need to hold you. Feel you breathing against me so I can be sure you are ok. I couldn't sleep. I was just lying there going over a million different ways that something could happen to you while I wasn't there. I was driving myself crazy."

"Well, I couldn't sleep either, so I understand. And having you in my bed, holding me, is going to get no complaints from me. The only place I feel safe right now is in your arms."

"I'll do everything in my power to keep you safe. Everything. I may have failed you once, but long as there is breath in my body, I will not fail you again. So, sleep. You can rest assured knowing that I am here and not a damn thing can touch you."

As I start drifting off to sleep, I can't help but think this is not how I thought my night would be ending. We have barely had any alone time together. I was beginning to think his declaration of love for me was a dream I had. So, him being here, feeling his breath sync with mine, is exactly what I needed to be reassured I wasn't crazy. Well, I may be a little crazy, but not in this instance.

Chapter 31

Well, my instincts were more or less correct. I got some sleep once my fight or flight response calmed the hell down after Jax scared the life out of me. I just kept waking up thinking about all the horrendous possibilities of what could happen to me if they managed to capture me this time. I'm not going to tell the boys that though. If they knew how anxious I really was about putting myself out there as bait, there is no way in hell they would go through with it.

So, while Jax is in the kitchen making some coffee, I put on a little makeup, that I normally don't use, to hide my black circles somewhat. After I'm mildly presentable I walk into the kitchen and slip my arms around Jax's waist from behind kissing his shoulder blade.

"Good morning." I hum.

He turns in my arms and kisses me on the top of my head. "Good morning, Kitten. The best morning I have had in a long time waking up next to you. How did you sleep?"

I give him the stink eye as I take my coffee he handed me and go sit at the bar to drink it.

"Well after my heart stopped trying to beat out of my chest it was nice."

He chuckles and grunts "sorry again".

"I got a lot more sleep than I thought I was going to. So, thank you for being here with me."

"Don't thank me. I want to be here. There's nowhere I'd rather be. I'd like to make this a regular thing. And maybe get some time to get to know each other once we aren't afraid for your life."

That thoughts makes my cheeks set on fire. I'd like to get to know him a hell of a lot more. Carnally. Yes please!

I think he's reading my mind again because he looks me up and down and chuckles to himself while he turns around to get back to whatever he's doing at the stove.

So, I just relax into my coffee and watch while I wait for the chaos brigade to get here. This is going to be a long exhausting day. I feel it already. 2 pots. This is going to be a 2 pot of coffee day.

I'm getting mentally prepared for all the arguing that's going to ensue when I hear the first door slam outside. My front door bursts open and without turning around I know that Paxton is the first to arrive.

"Goooooood morning Darlin'! Have you had your second cup of coffee yet? Or should I proceed with caution?"

He stops in his tracks when he sees Jaxson in my kitchen already. Still with bare feet. He starts to grin wildly and wiggle his eyebrows up and down.

"Oh brooooo! I was wondering where you got off to! Got off! Ha! I bet you did! Go big bro"!

Before I can even respond I hear the thwack of Paxton being smacked in the back of the head. Jax growls and tells him to

"Shut the fuck up before I kick your ass."

"Honestly Pax, I have no idea how you do not have a permanent concussion."

I hear him chuckle and feel a close presence behind me. Jaxson slides his hands on my waist and gently kisses the side of my neck. My whole body shudders. I still can't believe that he loves me.

"How are you today Jax?" I murmur. I realize he's been so focused on my well-being; no one has asked about his.

I get a grunt in response as he moves away to set his things on the kitchen table. That makes me chuckle. "That good huh?"

"Brother, I don't care whats going on, if I had a woman that beautiful smiling at me and giving me kisses there's no way anything could bring me down." Paxton throws out there, ever the unhelpful one.

"Hush your face Pax. He's stressed out so give him a break. "

Paxton instantly loses his smile and gets serious. "I know darlin' we're all a little stressed about what's about to go down."

Jax growls, "IF it goes down. I am still not convinced we can pull this off with 100% certainty she won't get hurt or taken."

And so it begins.

I walked up behind him and lay my head against his back. He stills instantly.

"We don't need to start arguing until everybody gets here. It won't do anybody any good."

He turns and wraps his arms round me and kisses the top of my head.

"I won't do anything to put you at risk. I won't. I just found you, I can't lose you."

Jax whispers into my hair. As I'm melting into a puddle of goo once again, I hear more car doors slam. The rest of the boys are here. Jax gently pulls away from me and straightens up. He went from soft and sweet to hard instantly. He's preparing for war. I sigh and walk back to the kitchen. More coffee it is then.

Paxton, Jaxson, Lindsey, and Eddy are all at my table now with the surface covered in computers, wires, maps, and a whole lot of other stuff that I couldn't even guess at what it is. So far, the conversation is moving smoothly and there isn't any confrontation yet. I can feel the tension though, so I know it's coming. I am at my kitchen counter bar with my paperwork looking over the final draft I wrote for the lawyer's preliminary statements and closing arguments for my court case.

I look up when I hear "Alright, it's time to iron out the details. We're going to go through every possible scenario that. We can think of, and I am going to think oof every possible way that it can go wrong. This will allow us to come up with the most full proof plan possible as well as back up plans."

Lindsey is going to be playing devil's advocate it seems. There's no way this could possibly go wrong. Cue mental eye roll. I already know Jaxson is about to get his panties in a wad. No way he's going to sit here quietly and listen to a million different scenarios of me getting attacked, whacked, and snatched.

Lindsey gives Jaxson a look.

"Are you ready for this?"

Jaxson's very predictable response is a growl and a hard no. Is it too early to switch to wine? Because I don't think coffee is going to cut it in this conversation. It's 5 o'clock somewhere, right? Paxton looks up to the ceiling and makes the sign of the cross.

Eddy chuckles to himself and says "Dios mio ayudanos por favor." I don't speak a whole lot of Spanish, but I guarantee I agree with his sentiment.

Lindsey slides over a large map into the center of the table. It has a large red circle on it. He begins with,

"The majority of the land is heavily wooded except for this area right here. I am making a calculated assumption that this is the location that they plan on using. It also works out to be the best location for US to use for our mission."

They all turn to look in my direction when I clear my throat. Paxton busts out laughing. Lindsey tries to cover his chuckle with a cough.

"Percy, you do not have to raise your hand. If you have a question, just ask."

"Sorry, but do we know what they are wanting to use this land for?"

Before Lindsey can answer me Jaxon quietly says "Kitten, you can put your hand down."

I'm pretty sure my face is 12 shades of red when I realize that I still have my hand in the air like an overachieving student trying to get their teacher's attention. I clear my throat again.

"Uh, sorry?"

Jaxson comes over to kiss the top of my head. "Don't apologize. It's cute."

"Ayyyyyyye, I never thought I would see the day when grizzly bear Jaxson gets a soft side!"

Eddy pipes up and is shaking his hand like he touched something hot.

"Mami I don't know what you are doing but you need to keep doing it. That's hot."

Jaxson throws a computer mouse at his head as he grumbles "shut the fuck up Eddy". Paxton is actually on the floor laughing and Lindsey has his face in his hand. Grumbling, "5 minutes in and it's already gone to shit." Now I'm red faced from trying not to laugh.

Lindsey continues, "Alright. Alright. Let's get back on track." He looks back at me, "with all the intel we have been gathering and piecing together, it looks like he is trying to get ahold of his property to move his operation to a more secluded location. With all the press on him recently he has too many eyes watching his every move. With him moving his base camp, so to speak, all the way out there he is hoping it will be an out of sight, out of mind kind of situation."

"That mother fucker. Defiling Mother Earth so he can off people in peace?!" I snap incredulously.

There's about a 3 second pause before they all bust out laughing in unison. Even Jaxson is laughing. Which makes me pause in my aggravation because that is the first time, I have ever seen him full on body laugh and it is a beautiful sight to see. As hot as he is when he is stoic, he completely transforms to drop dead gorgeous when he smiles.

"Ah Darlin' that is probably the cutest thing I have ever seen.

" Now I see why Jax calls you kitten because you taking your claws out is just adorable."

Paxton is still laughing when I try to throw my spoon at him but completely miss. He didn't even duck. I really need to work on my aim. This just makes him laugh even harder. He's full-blown bent over holding his stomach wheezing he is laughing at me so hard.

Jaxson comes over and soothes the frown on my face with his pointer finger and lifts my chin up so I can look at him.

"Ignore him kitten. He's a dumbass. But I do love this protective side, it makes me want to provoke you."

He winks at me and goes back over to his chair at the table. I think my insides quivered. Like actually quivered. I have heard that term being used before, but I didn't think it was an actual thing until just now. Yep. Quivering over here.

Lindsey tries again. "Yes Percy, you hit the nail on the head. He wants to build him an empire in the middle of nowhere so he can conduct his unsavory business out of the public eye. Which is why he is trying so hard to get rid of you so he can obtain it. You are in his way of expansion."

"Well good, fuck him." I huff.

Lindsey chuckles again as he turns back to the map. "Lucky for us, there is only one decent viable option right now to get to that clearing. That will make it a little easier to set up all the surveillance that we are going to need."

Eddy claps his hands and rubs them together. "It's my turn to shine!"

I smile to myself as I watch the guys start going over all their plans. It really is awesome watching their dynamic. I begin to like Eddy more and more while I watch them interact. He really does level out the team well by adding some light heartedness to the group. He was talking about me making Jaxson soft, but he didn't realize he makes them all loosen up a little with his smile and quick wit. It's interesting to watch how he brings them all back down when the conversation starts to get a little heated.

They start talking about logistics and strategies and I realize I am going to be no help for this conversation. As much as I want to be prepared as possible for what's to come, I really am just going to have to trust them that they will keep me safe and tell me what to do when the time is right.

Chapter 32

After days of listening to them nonstop strategize I am excited that have finally come to a resolution. My anxiety as at an all-time high sitting in The Toasted Almond to start the process of using me as bait. As much as I want this bullshit to be over with, I am also scared out of my mind that things won't go according to plan and it's going to end up very bad for me.

I trust the boys explicitly. I am not worried that they are not going to do everything in their power to make sure that things go off without a hitch. But I have seen the brutality that Russo and his men dole out on a regular basis. My shoulder still aches with constant reminder that he almost got what he wanted. When men like him have no morals and not an ounce of decency in them then the possibilities of mayhem are endless. His potential for torture and destruction is endless, and it's currently fully focused on me. Not a position that I am loving being in.

We know that they have eyes on me constantly, which is why I am sitting in my favorite place that I haven't been able to come to in forever. As happy as it would normally make me to be sitting here with Pax and Jax and enjoying the smell of fresh brewed coffee and fresh baked bread, we are here with a purpose.

We are the distractions. We want Russo's men to think that we have let our guard down and being stupid by discussing our plans out in the open. If they had half a brain cell, then they should probably question why all the sudden the boys have let me out of my cage that they have tightly kept me in since my shooting. It's going to work to our advantage though. While we are sitting here openly discussing the "plans" we have to try to draw Russo out of hiding, Lindsey and Eddy are at the clearing of we have chosen for our point of attack for lack of a better word. They are setting up all the trail cameras, trip wires, and other gadgets that they are using to be able to have the advantage.

I CAN'T WAIT FOR THIS to be over. I'm going to miss all the boys around all the time. They have really livened up my house. Jax's steady presence, Paxton's constant laughter, I'm even going to be Lindsey's stoicism, but I'm not going to miss the constant tension. The constantly having to look over my shoulder, the waiting for the boogeyman to jump out of the shadows. THAT I can get rid of and never have to deal with it again. Hopefully. That's the goal anyway.

My legs are bouncing so hard under the table that I'm pretty sure the baristas aren't going to want to give me anymore caffeine. My eyes are wandering constantly trying to see if I can pick out one of Russo's men, but they are doing a great job of blending. I'm only half listening to the boys loudly discussing the plans of Paxton taking me out to the clearing after lunch just me and him to go take some final pictures for my case.

Jaxson asks him if he wants him to go with him for extra protection, but Paxton is making a show out of mocking Russo. Saying it's not needed. That his henchman hasn't been successful in getting me yet with all their attempts so he's not worried. And they say I was poking the bear. Nothing like telling an egomaniac that he's not good at his job. Russo is for sure going to ramp it up now. I do a mental facepalm because I think he's laying it on a little thick.

"Pax. I think you need to tone it down a notch. We're trying to bait them, not make damn sure that they are going to torture me!" I whisper shout.

Jack kicks him under the table for good measure. "You're scary her dumbass. I think that's enough."

Paxton just winks at him. Like a job well done.

Chapter 33

It's go time. I take a deep breath. Whatever happens, happens. I'm going to leave it in the hands of the Universe and the boys to ensure that all goes smoothly. I'm oddly calm. The anticipation has been killing me but since it's finally time to make something happen, I feel like a weight has been lifted off my shoulders.

Jaxson walks behind me to whisper in my ear.

"It'll be ok Kitten. I've got you. I may have failed you once, but I swear on everything that I am that o will not fail you again. Whatever it takes. I'll die first before I let them take you from me."

He subtly kisses the top of my head while he walks out the door.

Paxton chuckles while I'm just staring at him blinking. It takes my brain a second to function again after his declaration.

I finally look at Paxton, "I don't want him to die for me. I don't want any of you to die for me."

"No one's going to die today Darlin.'"

"You don't know that!" I whisper yell.

"Well, true. Some of Russo's men are probably going to die", he winks at me, "but that's for us to worry about not you. It's unrealistic to think that no one is going to get injured in such a volatile situation. Even in the best-case scenario I highly doubt that it's not going to get intense. Both sides are willing to put it all on the line to get what we want." He shrugs at that. "The only thing you need to worry about is getting out of there alive and in one piece."

"If you think that's the only thing I'm going to worry about then you don't know me well at all. Besides the fact that I just may have found the love of my life in Jax, I care about you too. All of you. There's no way that I am going to be able to only think about myself."

"You're going to have to darlin'. You're going to have to trust us. Trust us with your life because that is what's on the line. We are trained for this. You are not. Believe me when I tell you that you are not just a job for us. We have all grown to care about it more than just a normal client, which is why we are all going to do everything in our power to make sure things go according to plan. Let us do what we do, but just in case we are all occupied, which they're going to try to do to single you out, you worry about you. Do whatever the hell you need to do to get away and get back to one of us."

I've never seen Paxton so serious. I guess this is weighing on him more than I realized. I just assumed since this is their literal job, it didn't really bother him too much. His reassurance is exactly what I need. I gave him a quick hug on the way out the door and then quickly steel my spine. Let's end this!

We're now in the car on the way to the clearing to set our trap. Which is funny because Russo must think we're walking into a trap. I wonder what it's going to feel like for him to be finally outsmarted. By a girl. I snort to myself. I hope that fucker gets knocked down a peg or two. Or gets caught and arrested and gets pegged for real. That makes me snort out loud and Paxton gives me a weird look. I just shake my head because I am sure he doesn't want to know what my current thought process is while he's trying to get his head in the game.

Before I know it, we are slowly pulling into the clear king. I take a deep breath at the same time that I notice I can not even see any of the preparations the boys have made out here. Which is amazing because I know there there. It gives me a boost of confidence because if I can't find them then Russo's henchmen won't see it coming either. I really hope they're feeling overly confident and don't send a whole army out here. We'll really be screwed. These guys are good, but they aren't superheroes. There's no way the 4 of them will be able to take on a whole army. Well, three of them. I'm not sure actually if Eddie is capable of fighting or if he's strictly just a tech guy. Guess I probably should have asked that question beforehand. I shrug to myself. Oh well it's too late now.

Paxton opens my door and lets me out of the car and is talking about the preparations they have planned as a ruse, but I'm not really listening. I know it doesn't really mean anything so my other senses are on high alert. It's silent out here. No birds chirping, no squirrels running through the brush. It's like the wildlife knows some shit is about to go down and they're making themselves scarce. It brings me back to the day I was shot. Right before the bullet hit me, I noticed the same thing happening.

Since my senses are on high alert, I hear the subtle sound of a branch snapping under someone's foot. Paxton stills instantly. He heard it too. He gestures to me to get behind the car and take cover. By the time I get back there and peek out the side of the car I see a shadow moving to the left. Starting to circle behind us. I throw a rock at Paxton to get his attention and he gives me a subtle nod that he notices too. I peeked out towards the right and saw another shadow coming around that way as well. My heart begins to pound.

Ok there's two of them so far. They were trying to sneak behind me to catch me off guard, so I slowly started making my around the car to get closer to Paxton. I don't feel like leaving myself alone at the back for them to grab me is a good idea. I'm keeping my back to the car, so I see anything coming at my front. By the time I make my way around to the front of the SUV someone is casually walking out of the tree line.

Holy shit. They really are confident in themselves. The man walking our way is none other than Russo himself. Paxton let's put a low whistle. "Well, they're bringing out the big guns today huh."

Russo chuckles darkly as he stops about halfway I to the clearing. Paxtons hand has moved subtly to gun at his hip and pushed me to his back with this other arm wrapped around me.

"For a big bad security team, you are not very smart" Russo tsks at Paxton. "Openly talking about your plans for all my men to hear. I was really hoping to be able to come up with a quick resolution and you just handed it to me on a silver platter. Out here all alone with my men surrounding you." He chuckles again darkly. "So just hand over the girl to me and I'll go on my way, and no one has to get hurt."

That makes me snort. "No one has to get hurt. You mean only me." Paxton's hold on me tightens a little like he's telling me to shut the hell up. I don't listen though, I'm here as bait so I'm going or bait him.

Russo waves in a c'est la vie expression. "Well, only you. But to me you are no one. Just a problem to be solved. An annoyance. I'm quite impressed that you have been as resilient as you are. I never would have thought a do good-er environmentalist would have it in her." He claps for me.

That just pisses me off. Fuck this narcissistic Italian asshole. All he's doing is lighting a fire in me to make damn sure we take his stupid ass down.

Paxton finally pipes up. "Oh no, what are we going to do." He says blandly. "What we're not going to do is hand her over to you. It'll be a cold day in hell before I let you take her with you. So kindly fuck right off."

That gets the smirk wiped off Russo's face. His expression turns deathly dark. He waved at his men. "I've had enough of this. Take her. Let's be done with mess."

On his que the two men behind us make a run for me. Paxton immediately whips his gun out of the holster and pushes me to the ground with my back to the bumper. He doesn't look at me at me, but he barks in my direction.

" Don't move!"

Fine by me! I plan on keeping my ass right here. He quickly takes out both men and I cover my ears from the loud ringing of the gun shots. Jesus! I don't remember that being so loud. I am not made for combat situations. My whole body begins to shake. I don't look over at the men that I hear dying in the dirt. Even with my ears covered I can hear the last rattle of their breath leaving their body.

Russo takes a step back as Paxton turns his gun on him. "Get down on the ground Russo!" Before he gets the last syllable out of his mouth more me come bursting out of the woods. Russo chuckles as he keeps backing up. "Good luck Paxton. I'm not so dumb to bring so few men with me then you think." As he disappears back into the tree line, he yells at his men to do whatever takes to get me and meet him back at the car.

With that his men burst forward and start running in our direction. I scream and cover my head because before they take two steps, one of them hit the ground. As soon as I have the thought that the boys must be using silencers, another body hits the ground. As I uncover my head when I finally realized that I am not being rushed, I see Russo slowly backing back up into the clearing. Jax has him at gun point. The look on Jax's face is clear to anyone who cares to look, that he is seriously having an internal battle. I have never seen him so furious. I can see that he wants to take him out and solve all our problems, but he's righteous enough that he knows he can't. That would make him just as bad as Russo.

Russo sees it also. "Ah, Jaxson, right? You don't want to do this."

"Oh, I very much do. This is all I've thought about since the first time one of your boys ran my girl off the road and tried to take her from me. There's nothing that I don't want to do more." Jaxson growls back at him.

There's a battle still raging on around me. Paxton is taking out men left no right, I'm assuming the sniper with the silencer is Lindsey. Russo's men are starting to scatter. They've realized that they walked right into a trap. My eyes are glued to Jaxson though, it's like the chaos around me has gone silent. I slowly stood up. An eery calm has washed over me. No matter how much this man has tried to ruin my life, tried to kidnap me, and kill me, I am not going to let him get the satisfaction of Jax's ruining his for some misguided sense of loyalty to me.

I slowly make my way across the clearing to get to Jaxson. I know he's struggling so I don't care how many bodies I must step over to get to him. I am going to make sure he doesn't throw his life away for me. My love for runs deep into my bones and I am not about to lose him to prison for this prick.

Even though Jaxson's eyes are string straight into Russo's soul, he still sees me inching closer. "Percy, what are you doing? Get the fuck out of here."

Eddy comes trotting into the clearing, "Aye muchachos! Back up is 3 minutes out! All we must do is hold the stragglers until then. Woo I can't believe that fucking worked! I was for sure we were going to get our asses hand to us." He chuckles as he goes to help Lindsey round up the leftovers of Russo's men who aren't dead or got away.

Russo opens his big mouth again. "You think you won? You think you can hold me? Nothing sticks to me. The second you hand me over my lawyer will have me out within the hour." He chuckles darkly. That makes Jaxson's finger twitch on the trigger of his gun.

Jaxson growls, "He's fucking right! They're just going to let him go Percy."

My hand touches the small of Jaxson back as I slide to get the handcuffs off his hip. Paxton has moved to stand guard behind Russo to make sure he doesn't have the chance to try to make an escape. "Not this time, Jax. There's no way he gets out of this one. We have irrefutable evidence against him." I calmly reply to him like I am talking to a skittish horse. I am afraid that one wrong thing said by Russo is going to have Jaxson throwing away his morality and just taking him out, and I refuse to let that happen. As much as I too want to see Russo go away for good, not at the risk of me losing Jaxson too.

So I slapped the cuffs on Russo and slowly ran my hand down Jaxson's arm holding the gun. His muscles are twitching, he is holding himself so tight. Right as I am about to try to reassure him again that we have him and he can back down, all hell breaks lose in the clearing, again. It suddenly is flooded with cops everywhere. I can't make sense of what's going on with all of them yelling at once to get down, put your hands up, get on the ground etc. The beams from scopes of rifles flashing back and forth like it's a disco. As I slowly raise my hands in compliances, slowly placing myself on the ground, the last thing I see is the smirk on Russo's face as he was being led away.

Chapter 34

After hours of irritatingly being asked the same questions over and over I was finally released from the interrogation room. I am surprised it took that long considering Olympus Security is a legitimate business. On the same side, I'm glad they are doing their due diligence considering how many dead bodies were left in the woods. Even if I am released, I am being released, it wouldn't make us any better than Russo if they just let us go after something like that.

No matter how many times I asked, they would not tell me anything about whether or not Russo has been released or is still being held. Contrary to what they wanted, that just made me shut down completely. You're not answering my questions? I'm not answering yours. To every question they asked of me I answered them the exact same way. There's a video of the whole event, watch it and you'll get the answers to everything. They didn't like that very much, but it took them a couple hours to finally give up and leave me alone.

As soon as I walked out of the interrogation room, Lindsey was in the lobby to greet me. Before he could open his mouth I anxiously asked,

"Where is Jaxson? Where is Pax? Why am I out but not them? They aren't keeping them are they!?"

Lindsey puts up his hand to silence me. "Take a breath Perc. Let me explain everything to you."

I take a deep breath and follow Lindsey out of the door of the police station. "Alright. I am calm. Get to explaining. Where is Jaxson and Paxton?"

Lindsey opens the door of one of their nondescript black SUV's and waits for me to be properly seated before he closes the door and walks around to get into the driver's side. He waits till he has pulled out into traffic to sigh.

"They are waiting for you at your house. I didn't want them sticking around here any longer than they needed to. I was afraid more questions would be thought of, and they would end up detained for longer. They're fine, you're fine, everything is fine."

He sighs again and whispers under his breath, "everything's fine and I can't believe that shit actually worked."

"The police interrogated them for as long as they did you. They answered everything to the truth. The police had no choice but to hold Russo. Thanks to Eddie and all his cameras set up, everything was on video. It is irrefutable evidence. We provided them with the entire case file that we have amassed against Russo. There is no chance in hell, no matter how good his lawyers are, for him to get away this time. We made sure there was an airtight case against him. The Police Chief all but kissed Jaxson because he has been trying to get something to pin on Russo for years."

"So, it's over? It's really over? "

"It's over."

All the tension seems to finally leave Lindsey's body. I think this might be the first time I have ever seen the man relax.

AFTER THAT ADMISSION it is pretty much silent for the rest of the way back to my house. Even though I know they are both fine, my leg will not stop bouncing in anxiousness. I just need to see him to make sure for myself. I need to get back to Jax and wrap my arms around him to be reassured everything is fine.

Before Lindsey even put the car in park I busted out of the car and running towards my door. Before I even get halfway there, my front door slams over and Jaxson is running to me. As soon as I am close enough, I launch myself at him. I wrap my legs around his waist, and he catches me easily. As I start sobbing onto his shoulder, he is rubbing his hand down my hair whispering.

"It's ok. Everyone is fine. It's over. Shhh" He kisses me on the top of my head.

"I know." I sniffle. "I just can't believe it's over. This has been the most insane several months of my life and I thought it was never going to end. I can't believe we won. I told that bastardized not to mess with me!"

Jaxson chuckles at that and sets me back on my feet and raises my chin to look at him. "You did Kitten. You won, and now we can move on." He hesitates a little. "Hopefully together. Now that we have that own of a bitch behind us, I would really like for us to get a fresh start. Really make a go at this. I am not ready to let you go."

"Yes! A million times yes! You're not getting rid of me anytime soon Mister. I am in this for the long haul."

"For as long as you will have me."

And he kisses the life out of me.

THE END

About the Author

Just a mom of 3 navigating this chaotic thing called life, trying to fulfill a life long dream. Sabrina has been a life long lover of all things literary and has always wanted to be able to participate. It has taken well into adulthood to finally accomplish those dreams and is a poster child for it's never too late!